The Clocks Of Iraz

Volume Two of **The Reluctant King**

L. Sprague de Camp

A Del Rey Book

BALLANTINE BOOKS • NEW YORK

To John and Ann Ashmead

Author's Note

While the reader may, naturally, pronounce the names in this tale as he pleases, for Penembic names I had the following scheme in mind: *ue* and *oe* as in German; *ui* (obscured) as in "biscuit"; other vowels more or less as in Spanish and consonants as in English. Hence Ayuir rhymes with "fire"; Chaluish, with "demolish"; Chui-vir, with "severe." The *h* in Sahmet, Fahramak is sounded: "sah-h'm-met," etc. The scheme is based upon the phonetics of Turkish.

CONTENTS

I	THE SCARLET MAMMOTH	1
II	THE FLYING FISH	20
III	THE TOWER OF KUMASHAR	38
IV	THE MASTER OF THE CLOCKS	55
V	THE TUNNEL OF HOSHCHA	69
VI	THE GOLEM GENERAL	88
VII	THE SIEGE OF IRAZ	111
VIII	THE BARBARIAN SAVIOR	125
IX	THE WAXEN WIFE	138
X	THE CROWN OF PENEMBEI	149

✠✠✠✠✠✠✠✠✠✠✠✠✠✠✠✠✠✠✠✠✠✠✠

I

THE
SCARLET MAMMOTH

It was the hour of the goat, on the thirteenth of the Month of the Unicorn, in the republic of Ir, one of the twelve city-states of Novaria.

In the tavern called the Scarlet Mammoth, in the city of Orynx, a slim, well-dressed young man toyed absently with a glass of wine and watched the door. Although this man wore Novarian garb, there was about him a suggestion of the exotic. His skin was darker than that of most Novarians, although the latter were a mainly brunet folk. Furthermore, his ornaments were gaudier than those of the Land of the Twelve Cities.

Across the common room sat an older man: a chunky fellow of medium height, with a plain, nondescript face, clad in garments of sober black. If the first man looked foppish, the second looked ostentatiously austere.

While the tall youth watched the door, the chunky man, now and then sipping from a leathern drinking jack of ale, watched the tall youth. Sweat beaded the foreheads of both men, for the weather was unseasonably hot.

The door flew open. In stamped six noisy, rough-looking men, covered with sweat and dust and cursing the heat. They seized the largest table in the common room and hammered on it. The tallest man, a burly, ruddy fellow with deep-set dark eyes under heavy black brows and a close-cut black beard, shouted:

"Ho, Theudus! Can't a gang of honest workmen get a drink, when their throats are caked with dust thick enough to raise a crop in?"

1

"Coming, coming, Master Nikko, if you'll stop that hellish racket," grumbled the taverner, appearing with his fists full of jacks of ale, a thick finger hooked around each handle. As he set the vessels down, he asked: "Be this your last day, working out of Orynx?"

"That's right," said the big man, across whose face a sword-cut had left a scar and put a kink in his nose. "We move to Evrodium on the morrow. Our orders are to make the aqueduct swing south, following the high ground, before reaching Ir City."

"I should think you'd cut directly across to Ir," said Theudus, "to shorten the total length."

"We would, but the Syndicate would have to pay for an arcade several leagues long, and you know how they are with money; they give it out as a glacier gives out heat. When the thing is built, they'll doubtless complain that the grade is too low and the channel clogs up. I warned 'em, but they wouldn't listen. No matter what route we pick, we poor surveyors get blamed."

"They've been talking about this project for years," said the taverner.

"Aye. They should have built it years agone, but I suppose they hoped that Zevatas would send enough rain to fill the old aqueducts. They did nought till water got so scarce that they had to ration baths. You ought to smell the air in that underground city! They could cut it up and sell it for fertilizer. Well, what's for dinner?"

As the men gave their orders, the slim young man approached the surveyors' table. Standing behind the big man, he rapped the latter on the shoulder with a peremptory forefinger. As the chief surveyor looked up, the younger man, speaking Novarian with an accent, said:

"You, there! Are you not Jorian of Ardamai?"

The big man's eyes narrowed, but his face remained blank and his voice level. "Never heard of him. I'm Nikko of Kortoli, as my mates here will attest."

"But that is—well, come over to my table, where we can talk."

"Certes, my unknown friend," said the surveyor in

2

no friendly tone. Carrying his ale, he rose and followed the other back to his table. He sat down beside the younger one, while his hand strayed to the knife at his belt. "Now, sir, what can I do for you?"

The other gave a high-pitched giggle. "Come, good my sir. Everyone has heard of Jorian of Ardamai, once king of Xylar, who fled his official decapitation and has been hiding—*ow*!"

"Be quiet," murmured the big man, who had slid an arm around the younger man's waist and then, with his other hand, had thrust his knife so that its point gently pricked the skin of the other's belly.

"How—how dare you!" cried the slim young man. "You cannot order me around! You durst not harm one of my rank!"

"Want to find out? An you'd not mess up Theudus' nice clean floor with your guts, you shall do exactly as told."

"B-but, my dear Jorian, I know you! Doctor Karadur said that Nikko of Kortoli was one of your false names, and that is how I tracked you hither—*eh*, stop that!"

"Then shut up, idiot! What has Karadur to do with this? Keep your voice down!"

"He gave me a letter to you—"

"Who are you, anyway?"

"M-my name is Zerlik son of Doerumik son of—"

"An uncouth name, if ever I heard one. Whence come you? Penembei?"

"Precisely, sir. The great city of Iraz, in fact. Now—"

"And Karadur is in Iraz?"

"Aye, Master Jor—*ow*!"

"The next time you speak that name aloud, I'll let you have it up to the hilt. Let's see this letter."

Zerlik looked down his long, hooked, high-bridged nose. "Really, sir, a gentleman like myself is not accustomed to such unmannerly—"

"The letter, your lordship, unless you want steel in your guts. Did Karadur hire you as messenger?"

"Really, good my sir! Persons of my quality do not work for pay. It is our duty to serve the court, and my

3

task is that of royal messenger. When His Majesty, knowing me fluent in Novarian, commanded me to bear Karadur's missive..."

During this speech, the big man had pried the seal off the letter and unfolded the sheet of reed paper. He frowned at the spidery writing on the crackly, golden-brown surface, then called:

"O Theudus! A candle, if you please."

When the candle had been brought, the big man read the following epistle:

> Karadur the Mulvanian to his stout comrade in the adventure of the Kist of Avlen, greetings.
>
> If you would recover your little Estrildis, and if you remember enough of your early training in clockmaking to put in order the clocks on the Tower of Kumashar, then come to Iraz with Master Zerlik. The task should not be difficult, for I understand that these clocks were installed by your sire in the first place. Farewell.

Jorian of Ardamai murmured: "The old fellow has better sense than you, Zerlik my boy. You'll notice he mentioned no names—"

He broke off as a movement on the other side of the room caught his eye. The man in plain, dark clothing laid a coin on his table, rose, and walked quietly out. Jorian caught a glimpse of his profile against the darkening sky, and then the door closed on the man.

"Theudus!" Jorian called.

"Aye, Master Nikko?"

"Who was that who just left?"

The taverner shrugged. "I know not. He's been here all afternoon, sipping a little ale and watching about him."

"Could you place him by his speech?"

"He said little; but what he said was, meseemed, with a southern accent."

Jorian grunted. "With those clothes and a southern accent, he has 'Xylar' written all over him, as surely as if he bore the crimson hourglass on his tunic."

4

"Are you not jumping to conclusions on scant evidence?" said Zerlik.

"Mayhap, but in my position one becomes sensitive to such things. If it make you happy, Master Zerlik, know that you're not the only stupid man in the room. I should have noticed this wight as soon as I came in, but I was thinking of other things."

"Mean you the Xylarians are still fain to cut your head off and throw it up for grabs, by way of choosing the next king? A beastly custom, I always thought."

"You'd find it even beastlier if it were your head. Well, I shall have to accept Karadur's invitation instanter. But travel costs money, and I have but little of the precious stuff."

"That is all right. Doctor Karadur entrusted me with a sum adequate for the purpose."

"Good. How came you hither?"

"In my chariot," said Zerlik.

"You drove all the way from Iraz? I knew not that the coastal road was good for wheeled traffic."

"It is not. My man and I had to dismount a hundred times, to manhandle the thing over rocks and out of holes. But we made it."

"Where is this man of yours?"

"Ayuir is in the kitchen. You would not expect him to dine with his master, would you?"

Jorian shrugged. After a pause, Zerlik said: "Well, sir, and what next?"

"I'm thinking. We have perhaps half an hour wherein to flee the Scarlet Mammoth ere a squad of Royal Guardsmen from Xylar arrives with nets and lariats. Are you staying here?"

"Aye. I have a private room. But surely you do not propose to leave tonight?"

"Yes I do, and forthwith."

"But my dinner!" cried Zerlik.

"Bugger your dinner; corpses have no appetite. If you hadn't blabbed my name... Anyway, command your man to hitch up your chariot whilst we gather our gear. What's your idea of whither we should go?"

"Why, back the way I came—through Xylar and along

the coastal road, at the foot of the Lograms, and down the coast to Penembei to Iraz."

Jorian shook his head grimly. "You'll never see me in Xylar—not whilst they seek to chop off my head."

"What, then? Shall we send eastward to Vindium and around the other end of the Lograms?"

"Not practical. 'Twould take months, and the valley of the Jhukna is wild, roadless land. Methinks we needs must go by sea."

"By sea!" Zerlik's voice rose to a squeak. "I hate the sea. Besides, what would become of my beautiful chariot?"

"You and your man can take it back the way you came. I'll join you in Iraz as soon as I can find passage."

"From what I hear, there is not much coastal shipping just now, with the pirates of Algarth active off the coast. Besides, I was commanded to accompany you, to render aid and assistance."

Jorian thought that if any help were called for, it would be he who rendered aid to this spoilt young fop rather than the other way round. But he merely said:

"Then come with me, whilst your man takes the chariot. If we cannot find passage on a coaster, we may have to sail our own ship, and that takes at least two."

"Ayuir might steal my car and run off with it!"

"That, young sir, is your problem."

"Nor can I be expected to flit about the world without a single attendant, like some wretched vagrant—"

"You'll learn, laddie. You'd be surprised what one can do when one puts one's mind to it." Jorian rose. "In any event, we cannot sit here havering all night. I go to pack and shall meet you back here in a quarter-hour. Tell your man to be ready to drive us down the river road to Chemnis." He stepped back to the large table and touched one of the surveyors on the arm. "Come up to the dormitory a moment, Ikadion."

With a puzzled frown, the other followed Jorian up the creaking stairs. In the dormitory, Jorian pulled his spare clothing, sword, and other possessions out from under the bed. He donned the scabbard and jammed the other gear into a stout canvas bag. As he worked he said:

"I fear I must run out on you, as the pard said to the lioness when the lion returned home."

"You mean—you mean to leave the gang?"

"Aye. That makes you head surveyor. The Syndicate owes me for the work I've done so far. Pray collect my pay and keep it against my return."

"When will that be, Nikko?"

"I know not. Perchance in a fortnight, perchance in a year."

"Whither away? Why the haste and mystery?"

"Say that I fear the blast of the wintry winds and the drip, drip, drip of the rain. When and if I return, I'll seek you out and tell you about it—and also collect my pay."

"The boys will be sorry to see you go. You drive them hard, but they think you're a good boss."

"'Tis good of you to say so. By rights you should have had my job."

"True, but I never could get the work out of them as you do. Did I hear that foreign fellow call you 'Jorian'?"

"Aye, but he had confused me with another man entirely."

With his duffel bag slung over his back and Ikadion following, Jorian strode to the head of the stair. Glancing over the scene below, he muttered: "Where's that Zerlik?" Then he stepped back and knocked on the door of the private room occupied by the Irazi.

"Coming, coming," said Zerlik's voice.

"Well, hurry up! Have you sent your man to get out the car?"

"Nay, Ayuir is in here helping me. You do not expect me to pack my own gear, do you?"

Jorian sucked his breath through his teeth. "I've just packed mine without dying of the effects. What do you want, an egg in your beer? Send the fellow out; we have no time to squander."

The door jerked open. Zerlik said: "My good man,

if you think I will do my own chores like a common lout, just to meet your convenience—"

Jorian flushed a dangerous red. At that moment, Zerlik's servant, a small, swarthy man, spoke timidly in his own tongue. Zerlik briefly replied. Ayuir picked up the massive wooden chest and issued from the room.

"One moment," said Zerlik. "I needs must give the room a last inspection, lest I forget aught."

Jorian waited while the servant staggered down the stairs with the chest. Ayuir set the box down near the door and scuttled out.

Zerlik came out of his room; he, Jorian, and Ikadion started down the stairs. As they did so, five men in plain black clothing entered the Scarlet Mammoth. In the lead came the chunky man, who pointed to Jorian and shouted:

"There he is, boys! Take him! King Jorian, I command you in the name of the kingdom of Xylar to surrender!"

The five rushed across the floor, circling around the table at which the gaping surveyors sat. As one of the former started up the stairs, Jorian swung his duffel bag off his shoulder and hurled it at the man. The missile bowled the fellow over, and the man behind him tripped over his body.

Before they could recover, Jorian's sword came out with a *wheep*. Jorian hurdled the two sprawling figures and brought the blade down in a whistling cut on the shoulder of the next intruder. The man screamed and staggered back, cloven halfway to the breastbone. He sank to the floor in a swiftly widening pool of blood.

Another black-clad man threw a net over Jorian's head. Jorian slashed at the net but only entangled his sword in its meshes. He struggled to tear off the net, but the men in black expertly drew it tighter about him, while one stepped up behind him with a bludgeon.

"Surveyors, to me," roared Jorian. "Help! Zerlik, bear a hand! Theudus!"

Coming out of their daze, the surveyors rose to attack the men in black. Three of the latter pulled out short swords. The surveyor had only daggers, but one picked up a stool and smote the nearest Xylarian over the head.

Theudus appeared with a mallet. After hesitating to see who was fighting whom, he waded in with the surveyors. Zerlik, after dancing excitedly about on the fringe of the fray, ran to his chest, fumbled with a key, opened the chest, and took out a light scimitar.

Assailed from all sides, the Xylarians left off cocooning Jorian to defend themselves. Jorian tore and cut his way out of the net and fell upon the foe. Since not only was he the largest man in the room but also his sword had much the longest reach, his reëntry into the fray tipped the odds against the kidnappers.

The combatants swayed back and forth, stabbing, punching, grappling, falling down and scrambling up again, hurling crockery, thrusting, slashing, swinging, and kicking. The room resounded with the shouts of the fighters, the boom of overturned furniture, and the crash of breaking tableware. Red blood spattered the floor and stained the fighters' garments. The Red Mammoth trembled to the stamping of feet. The din of roars, yells, curses, and threats wafted into the street, so that several Oryncians gathered about the door.

Outnumbered, the newcomers were soon overborne. Jorian sped a fierce thrust through the body of one, while the Xylarian was engaged with Zerlik. As the man fell, the remaining four set up a cry:

"Out! Flee! Save himself who can!"

The four burst through their opponents and out the door. Two dragged another, half-stunned by a blow from Theudus' mallet. The three still on their feet displayed slashed clothing and oozing wounds. The faces of two were masks of blood from head wounds. A flourish of weapons sent the spectators fleeing, and the quartet vanished into the gathering dark.

Inside, two surveyors bound up cuts, while Ikadion sat with head in hands, nursing a growing lump on his pate from a Xylarian bludgeon. The first man whom

Jorian had struck down was dead; the other coughed bloody froth.

"My nice tavern!" wailed Theudus, surveying the wreckage.

"We didn't do it wantonly, Master Theudus," said Jorian, leaning on his sword and breathing hard. "Bear a hand with cleaning up, Floro. You, too, Vilerias. Tot up the cost of breakage, mine host, and Master Zerlik will pay."

"What?" shrilled Zerlik.

"Charge it against the sum Karadur entrusted to you on my behalf."

"Are you in sooth the fugitive King Jorian of Xylar?" said a surveyor in an awed tone.

Jorian ignored the question and turned to Theudus, who stood over the wounded Xylarian. The taverner said:

"This fellow may linger for hours, but I misdoubt he'll survive. Someone should fetch the constable; there must be an inquest on these manslayings."

"Inquest all you like, but without me," said Jorian. "I'm off with Master Zerlik."

Theudus shook his head. "'Tis not lawful, to leave town ere the magistrate has dismissed you. There might be charges."

"I'm sorry. Whereas I am a reasonably law-abiding wight, I can't wait around for another gang to lay me by the heels, whilst your men of the law mumble gravely in their beards. Pay Master Theudus, O Zerlik." While Zerlik fumbled with his purse, Jorian donned his hat and shouldered his duffel bag. "Now let's forth!"

"But, Master Jorian!" said Zerlik. "It is all but dark."

"So much the better."

"But we shall get lost or overset the chariot—"

"Fear not; I'll drive. There's a moon, and I know the roads hereabouts."

Heavily laden with three men and their gear, Zerlik's chariot, drawn by a pair of handsome Fediruni whites, reached the village of Evrodium around midnight. Zerlik climbed down shakily, saying:

"Methought my last moment had come a hundred times, Master Jorian. Where got you that skill with driving a car?"

Jorian laughed. "I can do many things, some passing well and some not so well. I'm probably the only wandering adventurer especially trained for the rôle."

When they had secured quarters, Zerlik asked Jorian to elucidate his last remark. Over dinner, Jorian—who had a weakness for talk—explained.

"I got into the king business by happenstance. I was about your age and had been apprenticed to various crafts, such as clockmaking and carpentry, and had served a hitch in the army of Othomae. When that was over, I wandered into Xylar to see what might turn up. I happened upon the drill field outside Xylar City on the day of the casting of the Lot of Imbal, when they behead the old king and toss his head to the crowd.

"When, not knowing this curious custom, I saw this dark, round thing whirling towards me, I caught it without thinking. To my horror I found that I was the new king of Xylar, having caught my predecessor's gory head.

"As soon as I learnt that the same fate awaited me five years thence, I sought means to escape. I tried to flee, to bribe my way out, to persuade the Xylarians to change their damned system, and even to drink myself to death, all without avail.

"Then I learnt that, with the help of Doctor Karadur's spells, I might just possibly escape, in return for a favor I was able to do him. Did I succeed, howsomever, the Xylarians would pursue me to the ends of the earth, since their laws suffer not a new king to be chosen by any but the prescribed method, and therefore they must essay to drag me back and resume their interrupted rite to permit public business to go on."[*]

"How if the king die in office?" asked Zerlik. "Or if you die ere they can recapture you?"

"They have other procedures in such cases; but they

---

*See L. Sprague de Camp: *The Goblin Tower* (Pyramid Books, 1968).

11

are irrelevant to me, since I'm not yet dead and have no yearning to become so. To resume: Knowing that I was virtually condemned—should my escape succeed —to the life of a wandering adventurer, I prepared myself therefore by the practice of such arts as acting, rough-and-tumble fighting, sleight-of-hand, cozenage, and burglary. For these, I had the tutoring of some of the most unsavory rogues in the Twelve Cities. But some of their lessons have proven most serviceable."

Zerlik: "Do you like this irregulous life?"

"Nay. My real ambition is to be a respectable craftsman or tradesman—a surveyor, for ensample—earning a decent if modest living, rearing a family, meeting my obligations, and plaguing no man. A peaceful bourgeois life would suit me well, but it seems to flee before me like the end of a rainbow."

"If you knew the Xylarians were after you, why took you this post in Ir, next door to Xylar? Why not work in some more distant place, like Zolon or Tarxia?"

"Because the Xylarians hold something I wish: to wit, my wife. Therefore I skulk about their borders, seeking means to get her out."

"Oh. Is this the Estrildis whereof the letter from Karadur speaks?"

Jorian gave Zerlik a hard look. "By Imbal's iron pizzle, young sir, you seem to have made rather free with my private correspondence!"

"Oh, but Jorian, Doctor Karadur requested that I memorize the message, in case the letter were lost or destroyed!"

"Ah, that's different. Ay, 'tis she."

"Oh. I have heard that you Novarians entertain romantical notions about women. When one has several wives, as I have, one takes a particular woman less seriously."

"I had several wives, too, when I was king. Five, in fact; the Xylarians allow a plurality of wives to the king but not to his subjects. Mulvanian or Penembic influence in the southern tier, I suppose. But this was the last, and the one I chose myself."

"Really?" Zerlik patted a yawn. "It is hard for me to

imagine going to such trouble and risk over any woman. After all, they are all basically alike."

"I have not found them so."

Zerlik shrugged. "But why? It cannot be that you were otherwise condemned to a celibate life, for you Novarians seem to have no such rigid interdicts against fornication and adultery as, I am told, obtain among the Mulvanians. Is it that this woman is rich, and you wish to possess yourself of her property?"

"Not at all; she's a Kortolian farmer's daughter."

"Is she then of extraordinary beauty?"

"Not even that. She's a pretty little thing, with golden hair like a Shvenite; but of stocky build and too thick in the ankles to please the connoisseur of female beauty. No, Zerlik, it's what we call love."

"Oh, we have this 'love' amongst us, too. In our land, however, to fall in love is accounted a misfortune—a kind of madness. It leads men to entangle themselves with unsuitable women, causing their kin distress and embarrassment. Ordinarily, our parents choose our wives for us, very sensibly, by go-betweens, with the advice of astrologers and haruspices."

"This is not quite the same as your falling in love, laddie. Let me merely say that I enjoy Estrildis' company more than that of any other person I have known, and I am fain to have more of it, until death do us part."

"Well, I wish you joy of it. But does not one become bored with a single woman?"

"That depends. Having tried your system, I have no faith in it, either."

"How so?"

"There's a jingle that explains:

"Oh, pity the man with a score of wives!
For when they're at outs, however he strives
To gentle them down, the quarrel revives,
With curses and blows, and even with knives,
Till among them 'tis wonder that he survives.

"Oh, weep for the fellow with multiple mates!
For when they're in concord, with garrulous spates

13

Of chatter, they seek their desiderates
And wear him away by alternates,
Until the poor devil capitulates.

"Condole with the poor polygamist!
For every night he must keep a tryst
With one of the wives on the harem's list,
And he dare not repose or leave one unkissed,
Lest the peace of his family cease to exist."

"Whose verse is that?"

"An obscure poetaster, hight Jorian son of Evor. Anyway, one woman at a time's enough for me. When I get mine back, one wife, one house, and one honest trade will suffice me." Jorian yawned. "We must to bed, to be up ere dawn."

"But that will give us scarce four hours' sleep!"

"Aye, but Chemnis is a long day's drive hence."

"You mean to make Chemnis in one day?"

"Certes. Since four of those rogues escaped, the Xylarians will soon be on my trail again."

"You'll slay my poor horses!"

"I think not; and if I did, a self-proclaimed gentleman like you could afford another pair."

Beyond Evrodium, the road swung north to join the main road from Ir City to Chemnis, the main port of the republic at the mouth of the Kyamos. As Zerlik's chariot thundered down the river road to where Chemnis arose on the margin of the estuary, a forest of masts and yards loomed over the houses along the waterfront. Many ships had been laid up for the winter earlier than usual, since the depredations of the Algarthian pirates had depressed seaborne traffic.

The day after the arrival of Jorian and his companions in Chemnis, they walked to the waterfront in the early morning. Zerlik still staggered from the jolting of the previous day's headlong drive. Jorian growled:

"When I was king, we kept the sea thieves down. I built up our little fleet and commanded it myself. Betwixt us in the South and the navy of Zolon in the

North, no pirate dared to show his sail off the western coast of Novaria. But they've let the fleet go to the shipworms since I fled, whilst Zolon has a new High Admiral who dotes on fancy uniforms but never goes to sea."

Zerlik looked more and more unhappy. At last he said: "Master Jorian, I fear that when His Majesty sent me forth on this errand, he did not mean me to get my throat cut by pirates."

"Afraid?"

"Sirrah, a man of my rank does not brook insults!"

"Keep your doublet on, young fellow. I did but ask."

"I bloodied my scimitar on your side against the kidnappers. But meseems it were pure madness for us twain to set forth in some cockleshell craft alone. If these bloody freebooters caught up with us, what earthly chance should we have?"

Jorian frowned. "Well, no regular ships sail now to Iraz; so 'tis either buy or rent a ship of our own or not go at all. Rental were impractical, they say, for the owner would demand so large a deposit that one might as well buy the craft. Still, what you say makes sense of a sort.

"I have it! We'll be a pair of poor fishermen with but a meager catch to show for our pains." They reached the waterfront, and Jorian consulted a list of ships for sale. "Let's see; the *Divrunia* should lie yonder, with the *Flying Fish* beyond and the *Psaanius* in the other direction..."

Jorian hunted up a ship broker whose name he had. The broker took them on a tour of the waterfront. After a morning of inspecting ships, Jorian bid the broker farewell for the nonce. While he and Zerlik ate at a waterfront tavern, Jorian said:

"Meseems the *Flying Fish* is our craft, an we can beat Master Gatorix down to a reasonable price."

"That dirty little tub!" cried Zerlik. "Why—"

"You forget, laddie, that we shall be a pair of indigent fishers. So a craft like the *Divrunia*, as spick as a royal yacht, were the last thing we want. We must look the part."

15

"Well, the *Flying Fish* certainly stinks of fish. Why cannot we get a proper warship—say, one of those Irian biremes anchored out yonder? Then, with a well-armed crew, we should have nought to fear from corsairs."

"Imprimis, those galleys are the property of the Republic of Ir, and I have no reason to think the Syndicate would wish to sell one. Secundus, such a deal would at best require months of negotiation, during which time the Xylarians would be upon me. And tertius, have you a hundred thousand marks wherewith to buy the ship, with an equal amount for the hire of the crew?"

"Unh. But my good clothes—"

"We shall, naturally, wear garb suitable to our assumed rank. So fear not for your finery. We shall be ragged and stinking."

"Ugh!"

"Moreover, the *Flying Fish* is sound of hull and rigging. With her beam she may be slow, but she'll get us whither we fain would go. Finish your repast, so that we can sally forth to seek Master Gatorix."

When they found the ship broker again, Jorian said: "We should like another look at your *Flying Fish*; albeit a thousand marks is beyond the vault to heaven. Why, I could buy a surplus Zolonian trireme for that..."

After two hours of haggling, Jorian brought the price down to 650 marks. He said: "Methinks we can do business, Master Gatorix. Of course, you'll throw in a sun stone, a chart, and an astrolabe..."

After further chaffering, Jorian asked the broker about distances, winds, and currents between Chemnis and Iraz. Gatorix advised him that even with favorable weather, the voyage would take at least a sennight. Jorian calculated and dispatched Zerlik and Ayuir to buy supplies. When they returned, followed by longshoremen laden with sacks of biscuits, salt pork, apples, salted fish, salt, a fish net, two poles with lines and extra hooks, and suits of rough, worn seamen's garb, Jorian was again engrossed in an argument with Gatorix.

"I'm trying to get him to include this spyglass in the

deal," he explained. "He wants a hundred marks extra for the thing."

"Great Ughroluk!" cried Zerlik. "In Iraz, one can buy a good glass for a fraction of that."

"Naturally," said Gatorix, "since you Irazians invented the contraption and make it, 'tis cheaper there than here."

Jorian had raised the brass tube to his eye and trained it eastward. He stood silently for a moment, then closed the telescope with a snap and said in a changed voice:

"Pay Gatorix his hundred marks, Zerlik."

"But—"

"No buts! We're taking the glass without further argument."

"But—"

"And help me to get this stuff aboard, yarely."

"Surely, sirs," said Gatorix, "you're not putting to sea so late in the day?"

"No help for it," said Jorian. "Hop to it, Ayuir; you, too, Zerlik."

Between a quarter and a half of an hour later, the *Flying Fish* cast off and wallowed out into the estuary. The ship was a two-masted lateener, with a blue hull and yellow sails. She flew a large mainsail forward and a smaller mizzen aft. Seated abreast on the thwarts abaft the cabin, Jorian and Zerlik each heaved on an oar. Jorian had to exert only a fraction of his normal strength to keep the craft going in a straight line. He was so much stronger than Zerlik that, if he had put his back into it, he would have made the *Flying Fish* spin in circles.

As they drew away with exasperating slowness, Ayuir waved from the quay before disappearing towards their inn. The *Flying Fish* heaved and bounced on a brisk chop, driven up the estuary by a steady west wind. The afternoon sun blazed in a clear blue sky.

"I hope he makes it back to Penembei safely," said Zerlik in a worried tone. The young Irazi was already looking green. "He speaks but few words of Novarian."

"Poor fellow! I would have given him lessons."

17

"Oh, it is not with him that I am concerned, but with my beautiful car and team. I can always get another manservant."

Jorian grunted. Zerlik said: "Excuse me. I have heard of these curious ideals that are rife in Novaria, of consideration for the lower classes, and I suppose I should guard my tongue with more care. Why put we not up the sails now?"

"We ought to get farther from that lee shore first, lest this sea breeze blow us back thither and pile us up."

They rowed for a while in silence, until Zerlik said: "Let me rest for a moment; I am fordone."

"Very well. What sort of speech do you use in Penembei?"

"Why, Penembic, of course."

"Is it related to Fediruni? I speak fair Fediruni, as well as Mulvani and Shvenic."

"Nay; Penembic is related to no other tongue—at least, in this part of the world—albeit it contains not a few words of Fediruni and Novarian origin. Our dynasty is of remotely Fediruni origin, you know; King Juktar was a nomadic chieftain in Fedirun. And before that, a Novarian adventurer founded the city and begat a dynasty. But Penembic is a much more precise and logical tongue than your congeries of Novarian dialects. Most of us speak a little Fediruni, since that is the tongue of the cult of the supreme god Ughroluk."

"You must teach me Penembic."

"I shall be pleased to. At least it will take my mind off this damnable stench of fish. Tell me: Why took you Gatorix's exhorbitant price for his glass? And why the sudden haste?"

Jorian chuckled. "I looked through the telescope up the Kyamos and saw a squad of horsemen riding hard down the river road. They were mere specks in the glass, but natheless they gave the impression of Xylarian guardsmen...Hola!" Jorian reached behind him into the cabin and took the spyglass from its rack. He peered through it shoreward. "By Astis' ivory teats, those losels are on the quay now!"

18

"Let me see," said Zerlik.

On shore, the telescope showed a group of black-clad men, one of whom held the horses while the others expostulated with several Chemnites. Their vigorous gestures could be seen.

"Let's hope they don't find a barge and put to sea after us," muttered Jorian. "Eight oars could easily overhaul two. Row harder!"

After a while, Zerlik asked: "Could we not put up the sails now?"

"We shall, but count not too heavily upon them. With this onshore wind, we shall have to tack out to sea, and I know not how high our little tub will point. Here, give me the glass. Ten thousand demons, but they've already found a barge and are putting out! Now we're for it!"

✠✠✠✠✠✠✠✠✠✠✠✠✠✠✠✠✠

II

THE FLYING FISH

"WE MUST HOIST THE SAILS INSTANTER," SAID JORIAN.
Zerlik asked: "How do we that? I have never sailed."

"First, we heave to in the eye of the wind." With powerful strokes of his oar, Jorian turned the bow of the *Flying Fish* westward. The little ship pitched wildly as she took the waves bow-on. Jorian shipped his oar.

"Now," he said, "keep her in this position whilst I raise the sails. Oh, dip me in dung!"

"What is the matter?"

"I forgot that these sails had their covers on."

"I thought you were a nautical expert?"

"Do be quiet and let me think!" Jorian quickly unhooked the lashing of the mizzen cover.

"It is my skin, too," said Zerlik plaintively.

"Fear not for your precious skin. 'Tis I whom they're after."

"But if a fight develop, they will not draw subtle distinctions..."

Jorian, heaving on the mizzen halyard, forbore to answer. The mizzen yard went up by jerks. The yellow sail flapped and boomed as it luffed. Jorian shouted:

"Keep her head into the wind!"

"Why not sail on this sail alone?"

"Too far aft; she'd give us too much weather helm."

"I know not your nautical terms. Here come our pursuers!"

The black-hulled barge, rowed by eight men, had covered half the distance from the quay to the *Flying Fish*. Zerlik asked:

20

"Then why did you not put up that big front sail first?"

"One must hoist sail from stern forward. If one hoists the foremost sail first, the wind takes charge and sweeps one downwind—which in this case is upriver, whither we are fain not to go. There!"

Jorian belayed the halyard and worked his way forward to the mainmast. An instant later, Zerlik heard a wild yell. He called:

"What is the matter now?"

"May fiends torment, for a million eternities, the bastard who lashed this sail cover! He tied it in a hard knot, around to the front where I can't see it."

"Hasten, or the Xylarians will be upon us." The pursuers were now close enough for their faces to be discerned.

"I do my utmost. Shut up and hold her bow steady!"

The mainsail yard, swathed in the canvas sail cover, extended out for several feet beyond the bow. The knot that secured the lashing was at the forward end of this yard. To reach it, Jorian had to sprawl out lizardlike on the yard, gripping for dear life with his left arm, with his feet on the anchor, while he felt around the butt end of the yard with his free hand. To untie a hard knot with one hand takes doing even when one can see the knot, let alone when one has to work solely by touch.

The freshening wind drove larger and larger waves up the estuary. The *Flying Fish* leaped to each impact like a horse at a fence. Smash! smash! went the little ship's bow as she came down from each pitch.

Tossed up and down, eight or ten feet to each toss, Jorian had much ado to keep his grip on the yard. The sun, near to setting, turned the seaward waves to gold, which glared in Jorian's eyes like the glow from a furnace.

The barge drew closer. The Xylarians were within easy bowshot, but Jorian was sure they would not try archery. For one thing, the wind would carry their shafts awry; for another, they wanted him alive.

"Zevatas damn it!" he screamed as his hat blew off,

21

alighted gently on a wave, and went sailing up the estuary on its own.

"Jorian!" called Zerlik. "A man is readying a lariat."

When it seemed hopeless, Jorian felt the knot yield to his straining fingers. The black pursuing barge was almost within spitting distance. The knot came loose at last. Feverishly, Jorian unhooked the sail cover, bundled it up, and tossed it aft. It came down on Zerlik and wrapped itself pythonlike about him. In trying to free himself from the canvas, he let go his oar.

"Keep her head into the wind!" bellowed Jorian, heaving on the main halyard.

Zerlik bundled up the sail cover and returned his attention to his oar. "Here comes the noose!" he called.

One Xylarian cast his lariat, but the cast fell short, into the heaving blue water. The yellow mainsail went up. Its luffing in the strong wind shook the ship. Jorian shouted:

"Point her to starboard!"

"Which is that?"

"Oh, my gods! Back water, stupid!"

Zerlik caught a crab with his oar but at last did as commanded. As the bow fell off to starboard, the wind, with sharp cracks, filled the sails on the port tack. The *Flying Fish* heeled to starboard and began to pick up speed.

As Jorian scrambled aft, he saw that the Xylarian with the lariat was again whirling his noose. The man's black hood had fallen back, exposing a head of long, wheat-colored hair. The man, Jorian thought, was probably a nomad from the steppes of Shven. Xylar often hired these Northerners for the Royal Guard because of their skill with the lariat, since the principal duty of the Guard was, not to protect the king, but to keep him from escaping and to catch him alive if he tried.

This time, Jorian was within easy casting distance. He scuttled into the cockpit.

"Ship your oar," he said, "and catch hold of my belt in back."

"Why?"

"Just do it."

22

The oar clattered inboard. Jorian stood up in the cockpit, with one hand on the mizzen backstay, and thumbed his nose at the Xylarians. Zerlik caught his belt from behind. The Xylarian put one foot on his gunwale to make his cast.

Helped by the wind, the noose whirled through the air and settled around Jorian's shoulders. Jorian seized the rope in both hands and gave a mighty heave. Zerlik pulled at the same time. The Xylarian was jerked clear out of the barge, splash!

With cries of rage and alarm, the pursuers stopped rowing. Those on the near side of the barge rose and stretched out their oars to the man in the water. One, in his zeal, hit the swimmer over the head. The head vanished but soon bobbed up again.

The *Flying Fish* gained speed. Jorian crouched in the cockpit, holding the tiller with one hand and with the other, reeling in the rope. He grinned at Zerlik.

"One can never have too much good rope on shipboard," he said.

The barge fell astern, while the Xylarians hauled their dripping comrade aboard. Zerlik asked:

"Are we safe, now?"

"I know not. She seems to point pretty well on this tack; but we have yet to learn how featly she comes about and how well she pointed with the sails taken aback."

"What means that?"

Jorian explained the features of lateen sails and the good and bad points of shifting the yards to the leeward of the masts with each tack. He cast a worried glance ahead, where the far side of the estuary was opening out as they neared it: a long, low green line of marshes and woods, interspersed with croplands and villages.

"Get forward, Zerlik," he said, "and watch for shoal water. All we need now is to run aground."

"How shall I do that?"

"Look straight down and yell when you think you see bottom."

After a while, Jorian called a warning, put the helm sharply down, and brought the *Flying Fish* about on the starboard tack. The little ship responded well and pointed almost as high on this tack as on the other. Zerlik called:

"The Xylarians have not yet given up, O Jorian. They seek to cut us off."

Jorian shaded his eyes. Laboring into the teeth of the wind, the pursuers were forging seaward. Although the *Flying Fish* moved much faster than the barge, the angle at which the lateener was forced to sail by the direction of the wind brought the two vessels on converging courses.

"Should we not tack again, ere we come close?" asked Zerlik.

"Mayhap; but they'd still be south of us. They'd run farther out to sea and intercept us on the next tack. I have a better idea."

With a dangerous glint in his eye, Jorian held his course. Closer came the barge.

"Now," said Jorian, "take the trumpet, go forward, and shout a warning, that we mean to exercise our right of way. Let them stand off if they would not be run down."

"Jorian! The collision would smash both ships!"

"Do as I say!"

Shaking his head, Zerlik went forward and shouted his warning. The Xylarians turned faces towards the *Flying Fish*, swiftly bearing down upon them. There was motion aboard the craft as some of the pursuers readied their nets and lariats. The *Flying Fish* kept on.

"Can you swim, Zerlik?" asked Jorian.

"A little, but not from here to shore! My gods, Jorian, would you really ram them?"

"You shall see. Repeat your warning."

At the last minute, the barge burst into action. The rowers backed water, the sea foaming over their oars. The *Flying Fish* raced past so close to windward that the barge rocked in her wake. One Xylarian stood up to shake a fist until his comrades pulled him down again.

"*Whew!*" breathed Zerlik. "Would you have truly run them down?"

Jorian grinned. "You'll never know. But, with that much way on, 'twould not have been hard to dodge them. Anyway, we can now devote ourselves to the sea road to Iraz—if storms, calms, sea monsters, and pirates interfere not. Now excuse me whilst I pray to Psaan to avert these perils."

Night fell, but the brisk wind held. Having lost his lunch and being unable to eat any dinner, Zerlik sat moaning with his head in his hands.

"How do you stand it?" he asked, watching with revulsion as Jorian, one hand on the tiller, put away a hearty supper. "You eat enough for two."

Jorian bit a piece out of an apple, swallowed, and replied: "Oh, I used to get seasick, too. On my first cruise against pirates, as king of Xylar, I was sick as a dying dog. I was like that fellow in the operetta, *The Good Ship Petticoat*, by Galliben and Silfero—you know, the one who sings about being a pirate captain bold."

"I know it not. Could you give it to me?"

"I can try, albeit vocal training is one skill wherefore I've not had time." In a heavy bass voice, slightly off key, Jorian sang:

"Oh, I am a pirate captain bold;
I fill my vessel with jewels and gold
And slaughter my captives, young and old,
    To rule the raging sea, oh!

"And whether the blast be hot or cold,
And the tossing main be deep or shoaled,
I'm master of all that I behold
    As I cruise the ocean free, oh!

"But although with treasure I fill my hold,
And my loot at a bountiful price is sold,
I harbor a secret that's never been told:
    I'm sick as a dog at sea, oh!"

25

"That is good!" said Zerlik. "I would learn it; for I know no Novarian songs." He started off in a high but well-controlled tenor.

"You sing better than I ever shall," said Jorian after he had helped his comrade through the lyrics.

"Ah, but amongst us, to carry a tune well is deemed one of the accomplishments of a gentleman! How got you over your seasickness?"

"Well, thanks to Psaan—"

"Thanks to whom?"

"Psaan, the Novarian sea god. Anyway, my system adjusted, and I've never been seasick since. Perhaps you will adapt likewise. That reminds me: Is my—ah— colorful past known in Iraz?"

"Nay, at least so far as I know."

"Then how did you learn of it?"

"Doctor Karadur told me about your having been king of Xylar and accompanying him to Mulvan and Shven, to make it easier for me to find you. He swore me to secrecy, howsomever."

"Good for him! Karadur is a wise old man, if sometimes absent-minded. Now, when we reach your homeland, I want no word of my former kingship or aught else breathed abroad. To the Irazis I shall be merely a respectable technician. Do you understand?"

"Aye, sir."

"Then come hither and take the tiller. It must be the hour of the owl already, and I needs must get some sleep."

"May I run her closer to shore? I can barely see the coast, and so much water around me makes me nervous."

Zerlik gestured to eastward, where the Xylarian coast formed a black strip between sky and sea, both illuminated by the rising moon. The moon cast a million silvery spangles on the waves between the *Flying Fish* and the shore.

"Gods, no!" said Jorian. "Off a lee shore like this, the more water around us the better. Keep her as far from shore as we are now, and wake me if aught happens."

* * *

Next day, the west wind continued, blowing little cotton-wool clouds across the deep-blue sky. Zerlik still complained of headache but summoned enough strength to eat. Jorian, with a scarf tied around his head in piratical fashion in place of his lost hat, took the tiller. As he guided the *Flying Fish*, he quizzed Zerlik about the language of Penembei. After an hour of explanation, he clapped a hand to his forehead.

"Gods and goddesses!" he cried. "How do little Penembians ever master so complicated a tongue? I can understand having indicative, interrogative, imperative, conditional, and subjunctive moods; but when you add to those the optative, causative, dubitative, reportative, accelerative, narrative, continuative, and—"

"But of course, my good Jorian! That is why we deem our speech superior to all others, for one can say exactly what one means. Now, to go over the aorist perfect reportative of the verb 'to sleep' again. In Novarian you would say: 'They say that I used to sleep' but in Penembic we do all that with a single word—"

"A single word with fifty-three suffixes," growled Jorian. Later he said: "Perhaps you'd better merely teach me common expressions, like 'Good morning' and 'How much?' I used to think myself a fair linguist; but your grammar baffles me."

"Ah, but once you learn the rules, you have but to follow them to speak correctly. There is none of those irregularities and exceptions that make your Novarian tongue so maddening."

By mid-afternoon, the wind and the sea had moderated. Feeling better, Zerlik moved about, learning the spars, the lines, and the other parts of the ship.

"I shall be a true mariner yet!" he exclaimed in a rush of enthusiasm. Standing on the gunwale abeam of the mizzenmast, he burst into the song from *The Good Ship Petticoat*. As he reached the final "oh!" he let go the mizzen stay to make a dramatic gesture. At that instant, the *Flying Fish* lurched to a large wave. With a yell of dismay, Zerlik fell into the sea.

"By Vaisus' brazen arse!" cried Jorian as he put the helm down. The *Flying Fish* turned into the wind, lost way, and luffed. Jorian gathered up the rope he had taken from the Xylarians, belayed one end to a cleat, and hurled the rest of it to Zerlik, whose head bobbed into sight and out again with the rise and fall of the waves.

With the third cast, Zerlik got his hands on the rope. Jorian hauled him by the slack of his fisherman's blouse up over the counter. While Zerlik, bent into a knot of misery, retched, coughed, spat, and sneezed, Jorian said: "That'll teach you to keep a grip on something all the time you're out of the cockpit! Remember the rule: one hand for yourself, one for the ship."

"*Ghrlp,*" said Zerlik.

The wind fell. The sun set behind a bank of fog, which rolled in from the sea. Jorian said:

"We shall be becalmed in that fog. We'd better head into shore and anchor."

An hour later, as the first tendrils of fog drifted past the *Flying Fish*, Jorian dropped anchor and furled sail. The wind died. The waves became smooth little oily swells, just big enough to rock the *Flying Fish* gently. Jorian and Zerlik bailed out the bilge water with sponge and bucket.

When daylight vanished, utter darkness settled down, since the moon did not rise until hours after sunset. Jorian lit a small lanthorn. When he and his companion tired of language lessons, they played skillet by the feeble light. Jorian won several marks.

"Never bluff more than once at a sitting," he said. "Would you like me to take first watch?"

"Nay; I could not sleep, with all the salt water I have swallowed."

Later, Jorian was awakened. Zerlik whispered: "I hear something!"

Yawning and rubbing his eyes, Jorian ducked out of the cabin. A pearly opalescence in the fog showed that the moon had risen. The ocean was still as a pond, so that Jorian could not tell direction.

The sound was a rhythmic thump. Jorian, listening, said: "Galley oars."

"Whose galley?"

Jorian shrugged. "Belike Ir; belike Xylar; belike Algarthian pirates."

"What were the galleys of Ir or Xylar doing out in this murk?"

"I know not. The sea power of both states is at ebb—Ir because their pinchpenny Syndicate won't keep up their fleet; Xylar because they don't have me to keep 'em on their toes. Hence I surmise that all the ships of both are snug in harbor, and that the oars we hear are piratical."

"I should think the Algarthians would fear running aground as much as we do."

"They have wizards whose second sight enables them to warn their ships away from rocks and shoals. They can also see storms and fogs approaching from afar. Now let's be quiet, lest they hear us."

"A Penembic gentleman," muttered Zerlik, "would scorn to let such scum frighten him into silence."

"Be as knightly as you please, when you're on your own. Just now, 'tis my skin, too—as you remarked the other day. Since I am neither a Penembian nor a gentleman, I prefer saving my hide to parading my courage. Now shut up."

"You ought not to speak to me like that—" began Zerlik indignantly, but Jorian shot him so fierce a look that he subsided.

The sound of the oars grew louder. Mingled with them was the splash of the oar blades, the tap of the coxswain's drum, and an occasional snatch of speech. Jorian cocked an ear.

"I cannot quite make out their language," he breathed.

The sounds receded and died. Zerlik said: "May we speak, now?"

"I think so."

"Well, if these Algarthian wizards can foresee the weather, why cannot they control it?"

"Seeing is one thing; doing, quite another. There have been but few wizards who could control the winds and the waves, and their efforts have gone awry as often as not. Take the case of King Fusinian and the tides."

"What story is this?"

Jorian settled himself. "Fusinian was a former king of my native Kortoli. A son of Filoman the Well-Meaning, he was called Fusinian the Fox on account of his small stature, agility, and quickness of wit.

"Once, King Fusinian invited the leading members of his court to a picnic on the beach of Sigrum, a few leagues from Kortoli City, where the waves of the Inner Sea break on the silvery sands. A fine beach for picnicking, swimming, and like amusements it is. The beach lies in a long curve at the foot of a low bluff. Thither went Fusinian, with his lovely queen Thanuda and the royal children, and his high officers of state with their wives and children, too.

"Now, one of the guests was Fusinian's distant cousin Forvil, then enjoying a sinecure as curator of the royal art gallery. Being fat and lazy, Forvil impressed those who knew him—including the king—as a harmless nonentity. But the fact was that Forvil cherished royal ambitions of his own and, at the time of the picnic, had already begun to put forth tendrils of intrigue.

"In Fusinian's presence, however, the Honorable Forvil was full of unctuous flattery. This time he outdid himself, for he said: 'Your Majesty, your servants have placed the picnic chairs and tables where the rising tide will inundate us all.'

"'Really?' said Fusinian, staring. 'By Zevatas, I do believe you're right! I shall order all this gear moved to higher ground forthwith.'

"'Oh, sire, that will not be needed,' quoth Forvil. 'So great are Your Serene Majesty's powers that you have but to command the tides, and they will obey you.' For the tides in the Inner Sea, while smaller than those along this coast, are still big enough to drench a crew of picnickers who carelessly site their feast below the high-water mark."

"'Don't talk nonsense,' said Fusinian, and turned to give the command to move the chairs and tables.

"'Oh, but sire! 'Tis a simple fact!' persisted Forvil. 'An you believe me not, command the sea, and you shall see!'

"'Damn it, I will!' said Fusinian, no little annoyed, for he suspected that Forvil essayed to make a fool of him. 'And you, dear cousin, shall see what nugacities you are uttering.' So Fusinian stood up and waved his hands in mystic passes and cried:

> "Hocus pocus
> Keep your locus
> Do not soak us!"

"Then he sat down and resumed eating, saying: 'If we get wet, O Forvil, you shall pay for the damage to our raiment.'

"The guests likewise remained seated and ate, albeit nervously, since they did not wish on one hand to wet their finery, nor on the other to entreat their king discourteously by fleeing the tide whilst he faced it unflinching. And so things went for a time, whilst the picnic was consumed and the sweet wines were poured.

"But, strangely, the tide failed to rise at the appointed time. People looked surreptitiously at pocket sundials and at one another and—with deepening awe—at their lively little king, who ate and drank unconcerned. At last there was no doubt about it, that the tide had been halted in its wonted rise. Forvil stared at his king with his fat face the color of gypsum plaster.

"Fusinian was perturbed by this phenomenon, for he knew well enough that he had uttered no real magical spell, nor summoned a horde of demons to hold back the tide. And, whilst he pondered—keeping a straight face the whiles—one of his children approached him, saying: 'Daddy, a lady up on the hill asked us to give this to you.'

"Fusinian saw that the note was from the witch Gloé, who dwelt in the hills of southern Kortoli and had long coveted the post of chief magician of the kingdom. The fact was that she was not even a licensed wizardess, because of a long-standing feud betwixt her and Fusinian's Bureau of Commerce and Licenses. She had come uninvited to the picnic in hope of persuading King Fusinian to intervene with his bureaucrats. When, by her super-normal powers, she overheard the colloquy between Fusinian and Forvil, she seized the opportunity and, concealed in the woods above the bluff, cast her mightiest spell, to hold back the tide.

"Gloé's powers were, however, limited, as are those of all sentient beings. For most of an hour she held back the tide but then felt her authority weakening. She therefore scribbled this note and called to her the young prince, who was playing tag with the other children on the slope of the bluff. The note said: 'Gloé to His Majesty: Sire, my spell has slipped, and the waters are returning. Get you to higher ground.'

"Fusinian divined what had happened. But, if he confessed the truth, all the effect of retarding the tide would be lost, and Forvil would win this round. So he stood up and cried:

"'My friends, we have sat here gorging and swilling longer than is good for us. To settle our stomachs, I ordain a race to the top of yonder bluff. There shall be three classes: first, the children below the age of thirteen; the winner shall have a pony from the royal stables. Second: the ladies, for whom the prize shall be a silver tiara from the royal coffers. Third: the men, the swiftest of whom shall receive a crossbow from the royal armory. I warn you that I shall take part in the third race. Since, howsomever, 'twere ridiculous to award a prize to myself, I will, if I win, bestow it upon him who comes in second. Line up, children! Ready, set, go!' And the children were off like the wind in a yelling mob. Then he said: 'Line up, girls! You'd better hike those gowns up to the knee, if you would make any speed. Ready, set, go! And now, gentlemen...' And he repeated the performance with the men."

Zerlik put in: "If the king were competing, would not all the courtiers make a point of losing?"

"With some kings, aye; but not with Fusinian, whom

they knew to be a true sportsman. They knew that he would resent it if he caught anyone patronizing him by deliberately holding back. So they all ran their best. Being very wiry and active, Fusinian did in sooth reach the top of the bluff the first of the men. But poor Forvil, being fat, was puffing and waddling along at the base of the bluff when the tide came in with a rush, knocked him down, rolled him over, and half drowned him before a pair of servants pulled him out of the water.

"Fusinian always disclaimed any hand in the phenomenon of the tides, saying that it must have been the libration of the moon or some such thing. But his folk believed not these disclaimers and looked upon him with more awe than ever."

"Did he reward the witch?"

"Nay; for he said that she'd acted without authorization and, moreover, had given him a very uncomfortable time whilst trying to think his way out of the predicament into which she had plunged him. When he came down with a persistent itch on the soles of his feet, he suspected that Gloë in revenge had sent it upon him by goëtic magic. But nought could be proven; and his chief wizard, Doctor Aichos, managed to cure it."

"And the Honorable Forvil?"

"In consequence of these events, Fusinian entertained a lively suspicion of his cousin. Being Fusinian, he thought of an original way to discourage Forvil from hanging about the court and intriguing for power. Pretending that Forvil was a connoisseur of all the arts, he invited him down to the dungeon beneath his palace to listen to Fusinian practicing on his bagpipes. Forvil's perceptive criticisms of his playing, he said, would soon make him the finest piper in Novaria. After three days of this, Forvil 'got religion,' as they say, and became a priest of Astis. Thereafter his sacerdotal duties furnished him with a legitimate excuse for not listening to the howls of the royal instrument. In any case, he gave up his intrigues lest worse befall him."

An hour after sunrise, the fog thinned. A land breeze sprang up. The fog dissolved into patches and dwindled away; the sun blazed forth. Jorian hoisted the anchor and broke out the yellow sails. When they were well out to sea, Zerlik said:

"How convenient, that the wind should take us out to sea again when we wish to go thither! Did you pray to your Psaan?"

Jorian shook his head. "I like it not. A regular land breeze springs up at night and takes coasters and fishermen out to sea ere dawn. This feels like the kind of easter that heralds a storm...Murrain! Do I see ships off our starboard bow?"

Zerlik ducked around the mizzen. "Aye, that you do! One is a sailing ship; the other looks like some sort of galley but is also under sail."

"Take the tiller." Through the spyglass, Jorian examined the ships, which were bearing briskly down upon the *Flying Fish*. "Fry my balls, but I'm a dolt for not keeping a sharper watch! I ought to have seen them as soon as their mastheads showed. Now they've seen us."

"Pirates?"

"Indubitably. That blue thing they fly is the Algarthian flag."

"Can we flee?"

"No chance, curse it. If I knew the rocks and shoals hereabouts, I might seek refuge in water too shallow for them to follow; but I don't. If we had Karadur, belike he could cast a glamor on us to make us invisible, or at least to make us look like a rock in the sea. But we have him not."

"Why do the Twelve Cities not get together to extirpate this nuisance?"

"Because they're too busy quarreling amongst themselves, and one is ever hiring the pirates to plague another. Some years ago, in the reign of Tonio of Xylar, the Syndicate of Ir did hire the Zolonian navy to root the rascals out. But then the Novarians lapsed into their old ways, and the pirates sprang up in the archipelago again."

"You need an all-powerful emperor, like our king. What shall we do if they stop us?"

"We're humble fishermen, remember? Get a line over the side and troll."

The approaching ships were now near enough for details to be made out. One was a carack, converted from merchant service. The other had been a bireme, which now had her lower oar ports blocked to make her more serviceable in rough weather. Her oars had been shipped, but now several were thrust out through the upper ports on each side to add to her speed.

"I will not!" said Zerlik.

Jorian turned a puzzled frown. "Will not what?"

"Pretend to be a humble fisherman! I have been running and hiding ever since I met you, and I am sick of it. I will defy these scoundrels to do their worst!"

"Calm down, you idiot! You can't fight a whole shipload of freebooters."

"I care not!" cried Zerlik, becoming ever more excited. "At least, I shall take a few of these wretches with me!"

He ducked into the cabin and reappeared with his scimitar, which he unwrapped from its oilskin covering and drew from its sheath. He waved it at the approaching ships, forcing Jorian to duck to avoid getting slashed.

"Come on!" shrilled Zerlik. "I defy you! Come, and you shall taste the steel of a gentleman of—"

A heavy thump cut off his words, and he slumped to the floor of the cockpit, his sword clanging beside him. Jorian had struck him on the head with the heavy leaden ball forming the pommel of his dagger. He lashed the tiller, sheathed and put away the scimitar, got out the fishing tackle, and let a line trail a stern.

"Heave to!" came a shout through a speaking trumpet from the forecastle of the galley.

A sharp tug on Jorian's fishing pole told of a strike. He jerked the pole and felt a solid, quivering pull.

"Heave to, I said!" came the cry from the galley. "Are you fain to be run down?"

"Can ye na see that I've got a fish?" yelled Jorian, struggling with line and pole.

There was a buzz of talk on the galley. Some sportsman among the Algarthians was arguing that Jorian should be given a chance to land his catch before being pirated. The galley swung to starboard, backing water with her starboard oars. She furled her sail and rowed parallel to the *Flying Fish*, twenty paces away. The carack trimmed sail to follow more distantly.

Jorian landed a mackerel. Leaving the fish to flop in the bottom of the cockpit beside the unconscious Zerlik, he brought the *Flying Fish* into the wind and luffed.

"God den, me buckos, and what would ye with me?" he said in down-west Xylarian dialect. "Would ye buy some of me fish? There be this bonny fresh one ye seen me catch, and a dozen or three more salted in the hold. What would ye?"

More muttering on the galley. The man with the trumpet called: "We'll take your fish, Master Fisherman." As the galley maneuvered close to the *Flying Fish*, the man said: "What ails the other fellow, lying in the bilge?"

"Ah, the poor spalpeen—me nephew, he be—had no better sense than to try to drink the port dry, afore we cast off. So now he be as ye see him. He'll be jimp in an hour."

Someone on the galley lowered a basket on a line over the side. While several pirates with boathooks held the two vessels apart, Jorian tossed his fresh mackerel into the basket and followed it with salted fish from the hold. When the basket had been hoisted back aboard the galley, Jorian said:

"Now about me price..."

The pirate with the trumpet grinned over his rail. "Oh, we'll give you something vastly more precious than money."

"Eh? And what might that be?"

"Namely, your life. Farewell, Master Fisherman. Shove off!"

Jorian sat scowling up and moving his mouth in silent curses as the galley rowed away and broke out its sails. Then his scowl changed to a smile as he put his tiller to starboard, so that the little ship, as she backed before the shore wind, swung clockwise. The sails filled, and the *Flying Fish* resumed her southward course. Zerlik stirred, groaned, and pulled himself up on the thwart. He asked:

"What did you hit me with?"

Jorian unhooked his dagger from his belt. "See this? The blade won't come out unless you press this button. Hence I can use it as a bludgeon, holding the sheath and striking with this leaden pommel. I had one a couple of years ago, when I was adventuring with Karadur. I lost it later, but I liked the design so well that I had another made. It comes in handy when I wish, not to slay a man, but merely to stop him from doing something foolish—like getting my throat cut so that he can show what a fearless, gallant gentleman he is."

"I will get even with you for that blow, you insolent bully!"

"You'd better save your revenge until after we reach Iraz. I doubt if I could handle this craft alone; and if I could not, I'm sure you couldn't."

"Are you always so invincibly practical? Have you no human emotions? Are you a man or a machine of cogs and wires?"

Jorian chuckled. "Oh, I daresay I could make as big a fool of myself as the next, did I let myself go. When I was a young lad like you—"

"You are no doddering graybeard!"

"Forsooth, I'm not yet thirty; but the vicissitudes of an irregulous life have forced maturity upon me. If you're lucky, you will grow up fast, too, ere some childish blunder puts you into your next incarnation—as has almost happened thrice on this little voyage."

"Humph!" Zerlik ducked into the cabin, where he sat, holding his head and sulking, for the rest of the day.

Next day, however, he was cheerful again. He obeyed orders and performed his duties on the ship as if nothing had happened.

III

THE TOWER
OF KUMASHAR

For nearly a hundred leagues, the mighty Lograms marched along the western coast. The dragonspine of the range, clad in evergreen forests of somber hue, continued down into the sea. Hence, this part of the Western Ocean was spangled with islets and seawashed reefs and rocks, forcing ships to detour to seaward. Then the Lograms dwindled into the hills of Penembei, green in spring but a drab dun color, with only a faint speckling of green, in autumn.

As the sun arose above these green-spotted brown hills on the twenty-fourth of the Month of the Unicorn, Jorian aimed his spyglass southward along the coast. He said:

"Take a look, Zerlik. Is that your clock tower—that little thing that sticks up where the shoreline meets the horizon?"

Zerlik looked. "It could be...I do believe that it is...Aye, I see a plume of smoke from the top. That is the veritable Tower of Kumashar."

"Named for some former king, I suppose?"

"Nay, not so. It is a curious story as to how this came to pass."

"Say on."

"Know that Kumashar was an eminent architect and engineer, over a century ago in the reign of Shashtai the Third, otherwise called Shashtai the Crotchety. Now, Kumashar persuaded King Shashtai to hire him to build this lighthouse tower—without the clocks, however; those were installed later."

"I know," said Jorian. "My own dear father installed them when I was a little fellow."

"Really? Now that I think, I believe Karadur said something of that in this letter. Did your father take you to Iraz with him?"

"Nay; we dwelt in Ardamai, in Kortoli, and he was gone for several months on this contract. He claimed your king cheated him out of most of his fee, too; some confiscatory tax on money taken out of the kingdom. But go on with the tale."

"Well, King Shashtai wished his own name—not that of the architect—inscribed on the masonry for all to see. When Kumashar said that his name, too, ought to appear, the king waxed wroth. He told Kumashar that he was getting above himself and had better mend his ways.

"But Kumashar was not so easily balked. He built the tower with a shallow recess on one side, and on the masonry of the recess he personally chiseled: 'Erected by Kumashar the Son of Yuinda in the Two Hundred and Thirtieth Year of the Juktarian Dynasty.' Then he covered this inscription with a coating of plaster, flush with the rest of that side of the tower, and on the plaster he inscribed the name of the king as commanded.

"For some years, the tower bore the name of King Shashtai. But then the plaster softened in the brumal rains and peeled away, exposing the name of the architect.

"King Shashtai was furious when he learnt how he had been flouted. It would have gone hard with Kumashar had he not—fortunately or unfortunately, depending upon how one looks at it—already died of natural causes.

"So the king commanded that the offending inscription be chiseled out and one more to his liking substituted. But his officials had esteemed Kumashar highly and did not much like Shashtai the Crotchety, who was by this time old and infirm himself. So they politely acceded to the king's commands but then found endless pretexts for delaying the work. There was never quite enough money in the treasury, or unforeseen technical

39

problems had arisen, or something. And soon King Shashtai died in his turn, leaving the inscription still unmodified."

"Showing that the power even of these mighty monarchs is limited by human factors," said Jorian. "I went all through that as king of Xylar. 'Tis one thing to say to one's minion: 'Do this,' and have him reply: 'Yes, sire; I hear and obey'; and quite another to follow one's order down the chain of command and see that it be not mislaid along the way. What sort of king have you now?"

"King Ishabar?" Zerlik's features took on a stiff controlled expression. He gave a mechanical smile, such as Jorian had often seen on the faces of courtiers and officials during his own reign in Xylar. "Oh, sir, what a splendid monarch he is! Quite a paragon of wisdom, justice, courage, morality, prudence, dignity, generosity, and nobility."

"Sounds too good to be true. Has he *no* faults?"

"Ughroluk preserve us! Nay, not a fault. Of course, he *is* a bit of a gourmet. He sensibly devotes himself to the harmless pleasures of the table and leaves the details of running the state to experts, over whom he merely exercises a benevolent supervision. Moreoover, he is too prudent to risk his precious person by buzzing about the kingdom, forcing heavy expenses upon the locals to entertain him and upsetting the provincial officials and military commanders by importunate interference. Like a good king, he stays home in his palace and minds his business."

In other words, thought Jorian, the fellow is a lazy, self-indulgent hog who sits gorging in his gilded sty and lets the kingdom shift for itself.

The hills leveled off into the broad valley of the river Lyap, at the mouth of which sprawled vast Iraz. The *Flying Fish* sailed serenely past the suburb of Zaktan, on the northern side of the river. Zerlik pointed to a large, many-spired building, on whose gilded domes and turrets the midday sun flashed.

"The temple of Nubalyaga," he said.

"Who or what is Nubalyaga?"

"Our goddess of the moon and of love and fertility. The racecourse lies behind it. There is supposed to be a secret tunnel under the river, joining that temple with the royal palace. It is reported to have been dug at vast expense in the reign of King Hoshcha, to serve the king on the occasions of the Divine Marriage; but I know of none who will admit having actually seen it."

"If it ever existed, it must have filled up with water," said Jorian. "Those things always leak, and it would take an army with mops and buckets to keep it dry. But what's this Divine Marriage?"

"On the night of the full moon, the temple of Nubalyaga celebrates the wedding of Nubalyaga to Ughroluk, the god of the sun, of storms, and of war. The king plays the rôle of Ughroluk and the high priestess, that of Nubalyaga. Chaluish, the high priest of Ughroluk, and High Priestess Sahmet are nominally husband and wife, as required by their offices; but they have long been at bitter enmity, each trying to rape away some of the other's power. They fell out over the Prophecies of Salvation, a decade agone."

"What prophecies were these?"

"Oh, Sahmet announced that Nubalyaga had revealed to her in a dream that the salvation of Iraz depended on a barbarian savior from the North." Zerlik looked sharply at Jorian. "Would you qualify as a barbarian savior from the North?"

"Me? By Astis' ivory teats, no! I'm no barbarian, and I have all I can do to save my own hide, let alone a city's. But the other prophecy?"

"Well, not to be outdone, Chaluish proclaimed that all this about barbarian saviors was nonsense. His god Ughroluk had appeared to him in a trance and avouched that the salvation of Iraz depended on keeping the clocks in Kumashar's Tower running. And there things rest—albeit 'rest' is not the word I want, since the twain have continued to plot and intrigue against each other from that day to this."

They sailed past the mouth of the Lyap, where scores of ships, large and small, lay at anchor. There were high-

41

sided merchant galleons, smaller caracks and caravels, little coasters and fishermen, barges and wherries, and the long, low, lethal, black-hulled forms of war galleys. Preëminent among these were several huge catamarans, capable of carrying thousands of rowers, sailors, and marines in each twin-hulled ship. The sun gleamed on the gold-plated ornaments of the galleys. The Penembic flag, with a golden torch on a blue field, flew from their jackstaffs.

"I shouldn't think Algarthian pirates would venture near Iraz, in the face of that fleet," said Jorian.

Zerlik shrugged. "It is not, alas, so formidable as it looks."

"Wherefore so?"

"The costs of labor have been rising, so that His Majesty has been unable to afford full crews. And one of those monster double-hulled battleships, if its oars be not fully manned, is too slow and unwieldly to cope with pirates. There have in fact been several piracies within a few leagues of Iraz during the past year. Now there is talk of ships of black freebooters from Paalua, across the ocean, joining in the game. They once invaded Ir, did they not?"

"Aye, and not so long past."

The cries of sailormen came faintly across the water as some ships furled sails and were towed to their anchorages by tug-wherries. Others were towed out, broke out their sails, and put to sea.

The *Flying Fish* sailed past the river mouth and reached the waterfront of Iraz proper. Here, ships pushed off from the piers and quays, while others sought places at them, with much shouting and cursing.

Along the shore, wooden cranes slowly rotated and raised and lowered their loads, like long-necked water birds. They were powered by huge treadwheels, which in turn were manned by convicts. Behind them rose the sea wall guarding the city, and over the wall could be seen the domes and spires of Iraz. The hot sun flashed on roof plates of copper, or of copper plated with silver and gold. Beyond the city, on a ridge of higher ground, a row of windmills turned lazily in the gentle breeze.

"Where should we dock?" asked Jorian.

"I—I believe the fishing wharves are at the south end," said Zerlik.

The *Flying Fish* passed the Tower of Kumashar, soaring up over a furlong. Halfway up, on all four sides, the circle of a clock face interrupted the sweep of the buff-colored masonry. The single hand of all four clocks showed the Hour of the Otter. Jorian took out a ring with a short length of fine chain, held it suspended, and turned it slowly against the sun. A pinhole in the upper part of the ring let a tiny shaft of light through to illumine the hours marked on the inner side of the lower half of the ring.

"As I thought, 'tis past the Hour of the Turtle," said Jorian.

"If that be designed for measuring times in Ir," said Zerlik, "you must needs correct it for the distance you have come southward."

"I know that; but even with such a correction, 'tis plain that your clocks are out of order."

"They have not run for months. Old Yiyim, the clockmaster, kept saying that he would get them fixed any day. At length His Majesty lost patience. Doctor Karadur had been pressing him to let him take over the task, and now the king told him to go ahead. So the good doctor requested His Majesty to dispatch me to fetch you to Iraz. And behold, here we are! Excuse me whilst I don more seemly garb."

Zerlik vanished into the cabin, whence he presently emerged with a complete change of clothes. He wore a silken shirt with full sleeves and over it a short, embroidered, sleeveless vest. A knee-length pleated skirt clad his legs; slippers with turned-up toes, his feet. On his head sat the cylindrical, brimless, felt Irazi cap, like a small inverted bucket.

"You had better don your more respectable raiment, also," he said. "Even though you disclaim the status of gentleman, it were well as a practical matter to look like one."

"I daresay you're right," replied Jorian. In his turn,

he got out his one decent suit of shirt, jacket, hose tights, and soft boots.

"You are obviously a foreigner," said Zerlik, surveying him, "but that is no matter. Iraz is a cosmopolitan city, and the folk are used to exotic garb."

The *Flying Fish* came abreast of the fishing wharves, where nets spread like gigantic bats from house to house to dry. Jorian guided the little ship to within a score of yards of the first empty quay, then hove to and lowered the sails.

"Why sail we not right up to the mooring?" asked Zerlik. "It would make a better impression than laboring into shore by our oars, like a pair of base lumpers."

"If I knew the ship and the waterfront better, I might. As it is, I might miscalculate. Then we should smash into the quay and damage our ship. That would make a far worse impression than rowing."

As the *Flying Fish* touched gently against the quay, Jorian and Zerlik scrambled ashore and made fast to the bollards. While they were tying up, an official-looking person with brass buttons on his dark-blue vest and a short, curved sword at his side bustled up and spoke in Penembic. Zerlik answered. Although he could now make up a few simple sentences in the complex Penembic tongue, Jorian could not understand the language when spoken rapidly.

"He is a deputy port inspector," said Zerlik as the man climbed aboard the *Flying Fish*. "He will collect the harbor tax and issue you a temporary pass. Then you must apply at the Bureau of Travel and Immigration for a permit as a resident alien."

"Can we leave the ship tied up here?"

"I do not believe we are supposed to leave it overnight, but for a small bribe I think I can arrange it. He will not make things difficult for one of my rank."

"How shall I find Karadur?"

"Oh, I will take care of that. Instead of lugging our gear to our quarters like navvies, let you remain with the ship, guarding it, whilst I go to inform Doctor Karadur of our arrival. He will send transportation suitable for persons of our quality."

Jorian was not much taken with this plan, fearing being stranded in a strange city where he neither knew his way nor spoke the language. While he pondered his reply, the inspector sprang ashore again and chattered with Zerlik. Next, the inspector produced writing materials, including several small sheets of reed paper.

"He wants your name and nationality," said Zerlik.

With Zerlik translating, Jorian furnished the needed information, while the inspector filled in blanks on his form in duplicate. At last Jorian was asked to sign both copies.

"Will you kindly read this to me?" he said. "I like not to sign my name to aught I can't read; and your Penembic script looks like a tangle of fishhooks."

Zerlik translated the text: a statement of Jorian's identity, the purpose of his visit, and other elementary matters. At length he signed. The official handed him one copy and departed. Zerlik shouted across the waterfront street, and a donkey boy came running with his animal behind him.

"Farewell for the nonce!" cried Zerlik, swinging aboard the ass. "Guard well our impedimenta!"

He jogged off along the waterfront street, with the boy running beside him. Then he turned and vanished through one of the huge fortified gates in the sea wall, which rose behind the row of slatternly houses on the landward side of the street.

Jorian shaded his eyes against the low westering sun and gazed out to sea, which had become an undulating carpet of golden flakes. Then he examined his surroundings.

Men came and went along the waterfront. Most were Penembians in felt caps. Some wore a pleated knee-length skirt like Zerlik's, while others encased their legs in baggy trousers, gathered at the ankle. There was a sprinkling of Fedirunis in head cloths and robes, and an occasional Mulvanian in a bulbous turban. Now and then came a black man—a Paaluan with wavy hair and beard, wearing a feather cloak, or perhaps a kinky-haired, scar-faced man from the tropical jungles of Beraoti, swathed in animal skins or in a loosely-pinned rectangle of cloth. A train of laden camels swayed past, their bells chiming.

Jorian waited.

And he waited.

He took a turn along the waterfront, peering in the doors of the taverns and lodginghouses that backed against the sea wall and looking in shop windows. He tried to ask a few Irazis the way to Doctor Karadur's dwelling. He had put together the words comprising a simple question; but each time, the native came back with a long, rattling sentence, too fast for Jorian to understand. He stopped a man in a head cloth and queried him in Fediruni, but all the reply he got was:

"I am sorry, good sir, but I am a stranger here, too."

Jorian returned to the *Flying Fish* and waited some more. The sun set. He prepared a dinner from the supplies on the ship, ate, waited some more, and went to sleep in the cabin.

Next morning, there was still no sign of Zerlik. Jorian wondered whether the young man had fallen victim to an accident, or to foul play, or whether he had deliberately abandoned his companion.

Jorian would have liked to stroll about the neighborhood, to learn the layout of the nearby streets. On the other hand, he durst not leave his gear unguarded aboard the *Flying Fish*. Although the cabin door had a lock, it was of the sort that any enterprising thief could pick with a bent pin. To prove that this was the case, Jorian took out of a leathern inside pocket in his hose one of several pieces of bent wire and opened the locked door with ease. He had learnt to pick locks in preparing for his flight from Xylar.

To find a man in a strange city, without guide or map, where one did not speak the language, was a formidable task. (If he had known about street signs and house numbers, he would have added their lack to the hazards facing him. Never having heard of them, he did not miss them.) The task was perhaps not quite so hazardous as slaying a dragon or competing in spells with a first-class wizard, but it was still one to daunt all but the boldest.

When a merchantman pulled into a neighboring berth and several travelers stepped ashore, a tout hurried up to offer his services. Jorian, however, had a profound distrust of such gentry. The more eager one of them seemed to take the stranger in tow, the more likely he was to be planning robbery or murder.

The Hour of the Hare came, and Jorian still turned over plans. For instance, if he could accost a port official with whom he had some speech in common, he could then ask advice about trustworthy guides. Of course the fellow might hand him over to some cutthroat with whom he had an arrangement for sharing the loot...

As Jorian, seated in the cockpit of the *Flying Fish*, thought about these matters, a familiar figure appeared in the distance, ambling towards the *Flying Fish* on the back of an ass. It was a thin, dark-skinned old man with long white hair and beard, clad in a coarse brown robe and a bulbous white turban. He was followed by a youth mounted on another ass and leading a third.

Jorian bounded out of his ship. "Karadur!" he shouted.

The oldster drew rein and stiffly dismounted. Jorian folded him in a bearlike hug. Then they held each other out by the arms.

"By Imbal's brazen balls!" cried Jorian. "It's been over a year!"

"You look well, my son," said Karadur, on the middle finger of whose left hand shone a golden ring with a large, round, blue stone. "The sun has burnt you as dark as a black from the jungles of Beraoti."

"I've been conning this little tub for ten days, without a hat. And by the way, Holy Father, she's yours."

"What mean you, O Jorian?"

"The *Flying Fish* belongs to you. You furnished the wherewithal to buy her in Chemnis."

"Now, really, my son, what should I ever do with a ship like that? I am too old to take up fishing as a means of livelihood. So keep the ship; I relinquish her to you."

Jorian chuckled. "The same impractical old Karadur!

47

Well, I'm no fisherman, either, so perhaps your feelings won't be hurt if I sell her... On second thought, perhaps I had better keep her. When one becomes involved in one of your enterprises, one never knows when a speedy scape will be needed. But tell me: Where in the forty-nine Mulvanian hells is that ninny Zerlik? He was supposed to fetch me away yesterday."

Karadur shook his head. "A light-minded wight, I fear. I encountered him by happenstance this morn at the palace, whither he had come to deliver his report to the king. When he saw me, he clapped a hand to his forehead and cried: 'Oh, my gods, I forgot all about your friend Jorian! I left him awaiting me on the waterfront!' And then the tale came out."

"What had he been doing?"

"When he left you, he hastened home to greet his household and to see whether his charioteer had yet returned with his car and team. As it fell out, they had come in the day before; and so excited was Zerlik by the reunion with his beloved horses that he forgot about you."

"And also, I daresay, by the pleasant prospect of fut-tering his wives all night," said Jorian. "If I never see that young ass again, 'twill be too soon."

"Oh, but he greatly admires you! He talked me deaf about what a splendid comrade you were in a tight place: so masterful and omnicompetent. When you have completed your work here, if you embark upon another journey, he would fain accompany you, to play squire to your knight."

"'Tis good to know that someone esteems me, but he'd only be in the way. I suppose he is not a bad lad; just a damned fool. But then, I doubtless committed equal follies at his age. Now whither away? I need a bath."

"To my quarters, where you shall lodge. Put your bags on the spare ass, and we will deliver Zerlik's at his house on the way."

Over lunch at Karadur's apartment, in a rooming house near the palace, Jorian said: "As I understand it, you wish me to fix the clocks in the Tower of Kuma-shar, and this will somehow free Estrildis from Xylar. What's the connection?"

"My son, I have no instant method of recovering your spouse—"

"Then why haul me a hundred leagues down the coast? Of course, if the job pay well—"

"But I confidently expect to obtain such a method as a result of your success with the clocks. The little lady has not become some other's wife, has she?"

"I'm sure not. I got word to her by one of my brothers, who traveled through Xylar, selling and repairing clocks, and smuggled a note in to her. The note urged her, if she still loved me, to hold out; that I should find a way to bring her forth. But how will my repairing Irazi clocks do that?"

"It is thus. The high priest of Ughroluk once uttered a prophecy, that these clocks should save the city from destruction, provided that they were kept running on time. Last year the clocks stopped; nor could Clock-master Yiyim prevail upon them to function again. This is not surprising, since Yiyim was an impoverished cousin of the king, who had been appointed to this post because he was in penury and not because he knew aught about clocks."

"What's the state of the horological art in Iraz?"

"None exists, beyond a few water clocks imported from Novaria and the grand one that your father in-stalled in the tower. In the House of Learning, several savants strive to master the art. They have attained to the point where one of their clocks loses or gains no more than a quarter-hour a day. In a few years, me-thinks, Iraz will make clocks as good as any. Till then, the Irazis must make do with sundials, hourglasses, and time candles."

"What's this House of Learning?" asked Jorian.

"It is a great institution, set up over a century ago under—ah—who was that king?" Karadur snapped his fingers. "Drat it! My memory worsens every day. Ah! I remember: King Hoshcha. It has two divisions: the School of Spirit and the School of Matter. The former deals with the magical arts; the latter, with the mechanical arts. Each school includes libraries, laboratories, and classrooms wherein the savants impart their principles to students."

"Like the Academy at Othomae, but on a grander scale," said Jorian.

"Exactly, my son, exactly; save that the Academy— ah—devotes itself mainly to literary and theological studies, whereas the House of Learning deals with more utilitarian matters. I have a post in the School of Spirit."

"Come to think, I heard of this House when I was studying poetry at the Academy. Wasn't it they who developed the modern windmill?"

"Aye, it was. But the House of Learning is not what it was erstwhiles."

"How so?" asked Jorian.

"Hoshcha and his immediate successors were enthusiasts for the sciences, both material and spiritual. Under them, the House received lavish subsidies and achieved great advances. But later kings discovered that, for all the achievements of their laboratories, they were still bound by mortal limitations. A more efficient draft harness did not keep the king's officals from grafting and peculating and oppressing the people. A spell against smallpox did not cure the king of lusts, follies, and errors of judgment. An improved water wheel did not stop his kinsmen from trying to poison him to usurp the throne."

"If you fellows are given your heads, you'll have this world as mechanized as that afterworld, whither our souls go after death and where all tasks are done by machinery. You'll remember that I glimpsed it in my flight from Xylar."

Karadur shrugged and continued: "Discovering that life, even though materially better in some ways, was not really happier, the kings began to lose interest in the House of Learning. During the last half-century, appropriations have been steadily lessened. There have been no great advances since the invention of the telescope, thirty-odd years ago.

"The present head of the House of Learning is one

Borai—another sinecurist, unqualified for his task. Because of the prophecy concerning the clocks, the king and his advisers have been greatly exercised over their malfunction. The king has brought pressure to bear upon Borai, who in turn has brought it upon the dean of the School of Matter, who in his turn has applied it to Yiyim the Clockmaster—all to no avail.

"None of these gentlemen can admit the principle that appointments to the House of Learning ought to be on a basis of merit and knowledge, for then their own posts would be endangered. The expert, they assert, is too full of prejudices and convictions that this or that is impossible. Only the gentlemanly amateur can view these arcane arts in a judgmatical spirit. And so things have buzzed along for months, with much loquacity but no action.

"Last month, His Majesty gave a banquet to the professors of the School of Spirit. The king entertained us with such gustatory rarities as the tongues of the fatuliva bird of distant Burang—gods of Mulvan, how that man eats! Being myself a man of very simple tastes, I paid little heed to these exotic delicacies but seized the opportunity to broach some of my own ideas to His Majesty. I implied that, had I Borai's authority, I could eftsoons have his tower clocks put in order.

"We beat around the bush somewhat, since prudent commoners utter not blunt truths to kings, nor do wise kings reveal their full minds to commoners. King Ishbahar, howsomever, is not an unreasonable individual when one can get his mind off his stomach. He conceded that something must be done about his nontimekeeping timepieces. On the other hand, he could not simply dismiss Borai, who has powerful friends among the nobility, on the mere say-so of a junior professor and a foreigner at that.

"At last we reached a compromise. Ishbahar would grant me a special commission as Friend of the King, which in practice means king's errand boy. I might then make my own arrangements for fixing the clocks. If they worked, the king would pension off Borai and appoint me in his room. On the strength of my commis-

sion, I sent Zerlik to find you, having approximately
located you by divination."

"But how does this get my little darling out of that
gilded gaol in Xylar?"

"See you not, my son? As director of the House of
Learning, I can direct the efforts of the scientists and
magicians under my command in such directions as
would prove most efficacious in abducting your wife.
With all that intellectual power—"

"I wonder that you haven't figured out some magical
method of your own."

"That is not possible in my present situation. The
dean of the School of Spirit, Fahramak, is of the same
kidney as Borai and Yiyim. To make sure that I did
not—ah—'show him up,' as the vulgar put it, he as-
signed me to one of the most useless tasks he could
find: compiling a dictionary of the language of the demons of the Fifth Plane. He visits me betimes to make
certain that I waste not my time on other researches."

"What had you in mind as a method of rescue?"

"A magical flying vehicle seems the most promising.
You have certainly heard of flying brooms and carpets.
We have investigated these and found that, while it is
possible to imprison a demon in one of these objects
and compel him to bear it aloft, they leave much to be
desired as aërial vehicles."

"What do they do?"

"They wobble, overturn, go into a spin like that of
a falling leaf, and otherwise misbehave, with usually
fatal results for the would-be flier. Some of Fahramak's
savants are working on the problem now. If you will
repair the clocks, I shall be in a position to assign more
of my colleagues to the problem, and I doubt not that
we shall soon achieve our goal."

"Who will pay me," asked Jorian, "and how much?"

"I shall pay you from the fund set aside for my use
as King's Friend. Would half a Penembic royal a day
suit you?"

"How much is that in Novarian?"

"A Penembic royal is worth about two and a half
Irian marks, or a sixth of a Xylarian lion."

"Half a royal a day will do nicely, then."

"It is not so much as it seems at first blink, for these great cities are costly to dwell in. If you find yourself running short, confer with me."

"Meseems I shall do well to invest my first pay in some local garb, to be less conspicuous."

Karadur looked sharply. "That brings up a question. Dress has political significance here."

"*Oi!* How's that?"

"There are two racing factions, the Pants and the Kilts—"

"I beg your pardon. Said you racing factions?"

"Aye. Belike I had best begin at the beginning. Know that of all mankind, the folk of Iraz are the greatest sport fanatics, and their favorite sport is racing. They race beasts of divers kinds—even tortoises."

"What? Were a snail race not more thrilling?"

"Spare me your jests, my son. These are giant tortoises, from distant isles. Men ride them around the Hippodrome. Now there are two factions, distinguished by their garb. One faction wears kilts, like that which you saw on Master Zerlik; the other, trousers. It is a rare race that is not followed by a riot betwixt the factions, with knifings and other outrages; and there are affrays between factionists apart from the races."

"What's the political angle?"

"With so much rabid partisanship afloat, the factions have acquired political colorings. One might call the Pants the liberals and the Kilts the conservatives, since the kilt is the more traditional garment. Trews have come into fashion only in the last century, being copied from those worn in northern Mulvan."

"Then I shall perforce have to be enrolled as a liberal," said Jorian, "for I prefer trousers. Where stands the king in this?"

"He is supposed to be neutral, since the factions have public status and furnish companies of the Civic Guard. In fact, he leans to the Kilts, who are vociferous supporters of absolute monarchy, whereas the Pants would fain limit the king's power by an elective council. The Pants are in bad odor just now, for a dissident faction of them has fled Iraz, it is feared to foment revolt in the countryside. It were wiser for you, therefore, to dress as a Kilt."

Jorian stubbornly shook his head. "I shall wear trousers, for I should never feel comfortable in a skirt. Too drafty. You will have to explain that, as a foreigner, the garment has no political significance for me."

Karadur sighed. "I will try. As I said, King Ishbahar is not an unreasonable wight, if one interfere not with his gustatory pleasures."

IV

THE MASTER
OF THE CLOCKS

C LAD IN HIS BAGGY NEW IRAZI TROUSERS, JORIAN STOOD in the courtyard of the Tower of Kumashar and tipped his head back, squinting against the brightness of the sky.

"By Vaisus' brazen arse!" he said. "Those clocks must be thirty stories above us. Am I doomed to run up and down thirty flights of steps every day?"

"Nay, my son," said Karadur. "As the tower was originally built in the days of Shashtai the Third, men had to toil up all seventy-odd stories to bear fuel for the beacon. But so many workmen perished of heart failure that, when Joshcha established the House of Learning, he commanded the savants to devise a method of hoisting men and materials up and down the tower. Come with me, and you shall see."

The twain approached the vast entrance on the north side, where the huge teakwood doors were flanked and surmounted by sculptured lions, dragons, and gryphons. The soldier leaning against the stone of the door frame straightened up, stepped in front of the door, and clicked his greaves together as he came to attention. He barked a challenge in Penembic.

Karadur peered nearsightedly. "Oh," he said, and replied in the same tongue. "Here!"

The old Mulvanian produced a scroll of parchment, which he handed to the soldier. The latter, needing both hands to unroll the stiff sheet, had to balance his halberd awkwardly in the crook of his arm as he read. He

55

let the parchment roll up again with a snap and handed it back.

"Pass, sirs!" he said, bringing his fist up to his bronzen breastplate in salute. He turned the big brass door handle with a clank and pushed open one of the teakwood valves. The hinges squealed.

The interior was cavernous and dusty. After the brilliance of the sun outside, it seemed dark, although windows at every story let in light. The light was dimmed, however, by the dirt on the windowpanes.

To the right, the main staircase rose from the floor. It circled round and round the tower as it rose, with landings at every story to give access to the many small chambers built into the structure. The hollow shaft of the interior rose into dimness far above.

On the ground floor were pieces of apparatus: chains and ropes hanging down from above and, to one side, a horse mill. This comprised a vertical shaft with a horizontal crosspiece on top. From each end of the crosspiece dangled a set of straps and a horse collar. No animals now occupied the harness.

"What's that?" asked Jorian.

"When the clocks are running, the water that drives them must needs be daily pumped from the sump back up into the reservoir. A pair of mules, attached to yon mill, turns the shaft, which drives the pump by means of those chains and sprockets and things. You would understand them better than I. Since the clocks have stopped, howsomever, the mules have been put to other tasks. Hola, Saghol!"

A bundle of rags in a corner stirred and resolved itself into a sleeping workman. As the man rose, a grin split the brown face and showed an irregular row of yellow teeth.

"Ah, Doctor Karadur!" said the man and went on in Penembic. Jorian thought he said: "Do you wish to go up?"

"Aye," said Karadur and turned to Jorian. "How much do you weigh, my son?"

"A hundred and ninety the last time I weighed. When I get over two hundred, I begin to worry. Why?"

"Your weight must be counterbalanced." Karadur turned to the lift attendant. "Allow us three hundred and a quarter."

Saghol pulled one of the cords that hung from above, whence a bell tinkled faintly.

"Stand in this thing with me," said Karadur. The wizard stepped into a large, open-topped wooden box or tray, six feet on a side, with a handrail around it and a gantrylike structure arching over their heads. Attached to this structure was a chain, which extended upward out of sight.

Saghol grasped another cord and jerked it thirteen times, with a pause between jerks. Then he pulled the first cord again, twice. The bell tinkled.

"Whatever is he doing?" asked Jorian.

"He is signaling his colleagues above to set counterweights weighing three hundred and twenty-five pounds in the other car, to balance our weight. Hold tight!"

Jorian gripped the stanchion on his side of the box, which trembled and rose. "By Zevatas' golden whiskers!" he exclaimed as he peered over the edge.

"Make no sharp movements," said Karadur, "lest you set this car to swinging like a pendulum."

The stairs and chambers of the tower sank past as the lift rose. The walls came slowly closer, since the tower tapered upward. At the sixteenth story, the other car, laden with cast-iron weights, sank past them. The sounds of gearwheels and ratchets from above waxed louder.

The car stopped, and Karadur stepped briskly out. Jorian followed. A pair of brawny, sweating Irazis rested from turning a pair of large flywheels by means of crank handles.

The shaft bearing these wheels was united by gearing with a huge sprocket wheel mounted over the center of the hollow shaft of the tower. The lift car that had carried Jorian up hung from one end of the chain that passed over the sprocket, while the weighted car that had passed them hung from the other. A dog locked the gearing in place.

"*Whew!*" said Jorian, peering uneasily down the shaft. "That scared me worse than when the princess Yargali turned into a monster serpent whilst I was in bed with her."

"Now, now, my son!" said Karadur. "Do you still practise your old vice of self-deprecation?"

Jorian grinned weakly. "Not very often, Holy Father. Anyway, I misdoubt these fellows understand Novarian." He stepped to one of the windows. Beneath him, vast Iraz lay spread out, with broad, straight processional avenues cutting at various angles through the tangle of lesser streets and alleys. Amid the sea of red-tiled roofs, the metallic roof-plates of temples and other public buildings flashed blindingly in the sunlight, like gems scattered about a red-patterned counterpane.

"*Oi!*" said Jorian. "Karadur, tell me: is that the palace? And that the temple of Ughroluk? And that the House of Learning? Where lies our tenement?"

Karadur pointed out landmarks. Jorian said: "I wonder the king add not a few coppers to his treasury by letting the vulgus up the tower for a small fee, to enjoy the view."

"One of Ishbahar's predecessors did that; but so many young people, disappointed in love, ascended the tower to jump from the top that the privilege was rescinded. If you have seen enough, follow me."

The old man led Jorian up a narrow stair to the next level, cluttered by a mass of machinery. To one side rose another lift, like the one that had brought them halfway up the tower but smaller.

"That takes fuel up to the beacon," said Karadur. "There is Yiyim now."

A metallic tapping came from the clockwork. Then a small, gnomish man with a graying beard popped out of the gearing. In one hand he gripped a hammer, with which he had been tapping one of the huge brass gearwheels.

"O Yiyim," said Karadur, "this is Jorian the Kortolian, whom the king has commanded to repair the clocks. Jorian, I present Clockmaster Yiyim."

Yiyim stood glaring with fists on hips, silent but for

the hiss of breath in his nostrils. Then he hurled his hammer to the floor with a clang.

"You cursed old pickthank!" he screeched. "Offspring of a demon and a sow! Incondite meddler!" He added several more epithets, for which Jorian's limited Penembic was inadequate. "So your plot finally came to a boil, eh? And you think I'll show this young mountebank how these clocks work, so that he can steal the credit for starting them and cozen me out of my post, eh? Well, not one word of help shall you have from me! If the twain of you get caught in the gears and ground to sausage, so much the better. May the gods piss on you!"

Yiyim vanished down the stairs. The sounds of the lift told of his departure.

"Something tells me I had better not stand at the base of the tower whilst that fellow's at the top," said Jorian, "where he could drop something on me."

"Oh, he is harmless. If you succeed, Ishbahar will pension him off; and he surely would not risk loss of his pension by fomenting trouble."

"Yes? Umm. I've seen what happened before when you trusted somebody to be upright and reasonable." Jorian picked up the hammer. "Here's one tool, anyway. There's a tool rack on yonder wall, but with nary a tool in it."

"They have all been mislaid or purloined over the years," said Karadur. "You needs must furnish your own."

"I shall, when I've looked over the works..."

For an hour, Karadur sat cross-legged on the floor, absorbed in meditation, while Jorian tapped and pried and fingered the clockwork. At last he said:

"I haven't worked on clocks for years, but it is plain as your whiskers why this machine won't run."

"What is the cause, my son?"

"Causes, you mean. For one thing, one of the pallets of the escapement is bent. For another, somebody must have struck this gear in the train a heavy blow and marred one of the teeth. For three, the oil in the bearings

59

has been allowed to dry and get sticky, so the wheels wouldn't turn even if all the other faults were righted."

"Can you rectify these deficiencies?"

"I think so. But first I must order tools. Who would be the best man in Iraz for that?"

On the twenty-third of the Month of the Stag, a procession arrived at the courtyard of the Tower of Ku-mashar. First marched a musical band. Then came a company of the royal guard, consisting of one platoon each of pikemen, swordsmen, and arbalesters. Then came the royal litter, borne on the shoulders, not of slaves, but of the leading gentlemen of the court, half of them in kilts and half in trousers. A squadron of cavalry brought up the rear.

The courtiers set down the litter in front of the main entrance. As the curtains of the litter parted, the soldiers clanged to salute, while the civilians dropped to one knee.

An enormously fat man in a gold-embroidered white robe, with a curly wig on his head and a serpent crown on top of that, emerged slowly from the litter. The effort made him puff and wheeze.

When King Ishbahar had caught his breath, he made an upward gesture, so that the sun flashed on the huge ruby seal stone on the middle finger of his left hand. In a high, wheezy voice he said:

"Rise, good people! Ah, Doctor Karadur!"

The king waddled forward. In his path lay a puddle from yesterday's rain, but one of the gentlemen quickly threw his mantle over it.

Karadur bowed. The king said: "And is this your young—ah—Master—ah—"

"Jorian, Your Majesty," said Karadur.

"Master Jorian? A pleasure to know you, young sir, heh heh. Are the clocks running?"

"Aye, O King," said Jorian. "Would you fain see the works?"

"Indeed we would. Is the lift working?"

"Aye, sire."

"We trust all its parts are sound and solid, for we are not exactly a sylph, heh heh! Let us go; let us go."

The king puffed his way through the portal. Inside, the ground floor of the tower had received a hasty sweeping and cleaning. A pair of mules walked the boom of the mill around, while a muleteer from time to time cut at one or the other with his whip. The gears and shafting grumbled. The king stepped aboard the lift.

"Doctor Karadur!" he said. "It were inconsiderate to ask one of your years to climb thirty flights, so you shall ride with us. You, too, Master Jorian, to answer technical questions."

"Your Majesty!" said one of the gentlemen—a tall, thin man with a pointed gray beard. "No offense to Messires Karadur and Jorian, but it were risky to entrust yourself to the car without a bodyguard."

"Well, heh heh, one stalwart soldier ought to suffice."

"If lift will bear weight, sire," said Jorian.

"What is its limit?"

"I know not for sure, but methinks we press it."

"Ah, well, we cannot diet down in time for this ride. Colonel Chuivir!"

"Aye, sire?" replied the most glittering soldier of all, a strikingly handsome man as tall as Jorian.

"Detail a squad of the guard to ascend the tower by the stairs, keeping on a level with us as the lift bears us aloft. Pick strong men with sound hearts! We would not have them collapse halfway up, heh heh."

Like the tower, Saghol, the ground-floor lift attendant, had been cleaned up for the occasion. He jerked his cords, and the lift rose, groaning. The squad of guardsmen clattered up the stairs, keeping pace with the lift.

At the top, the king got off the lift, which wobbled as his weight left it, and wheezed his way up to the clockwork floor. Jorian followed. The soldiers, red-faced, sweating, and gasping, filed into the clockwork chamber after him.

On the clockwork floor, the machinery was in full noisy operation. The shaft driven by the horse mill on the ground floor rotated, driving the pump that raised water from the sump to the reservoir above. Water ran from this reservoir through a pipe to a large wheel bearing a circle of buckets. As each bucket filled, the escapement released the wheel, allowing it to rotate just far enough to bring an empty bucket under the spout. At the bottom of their travel, the buckets tipped, spilling their water into the trough, whence it ran to the sump. The bucket wheel drove a gear train connected to the shafts of the four clocks on the four sides of the tower. Another mechanism struck a gong on the hour.

"We have not been up here in years, heh, heh," said King Ishbahar, raising his voice to be heard above the clatter and splashing. "Pray explain this to me, good Master Jorian."

Jorian's Penembic was now fairly fluent if ungrammatical. With Karadur helping to translate when he got stuck, Jorian told the king about clockwork. While Jorian spoke, several gentlemen, having come up on the second trip of the lift, filed into the chamber.

"You should know Doctor Borai, O Jorian," said the King. "He is director of our House of Learning—at least for now."

Borai, potbellied, gray-bearded, and kilted, bowed to Jorian, mumbled something that Jorian could not hear, and shot a slit-eyed glare at Karadur.

"Pardon us a moment," said the king. "We would speak to him of plans for the city, and where better to discuss such things than this lofty eyrie, whence it is spread out below us like a map?"

The king waddled over to a window, where to Borai he pointed out various things below, talking animatedly. A plump, trousered man a little older than Jorian addressed him.

"Permit me, Master Jorian. I am Lord Vegh, stasiarch of the Pants. I see by your garb that you are a person of progressive ideas, like those of my honorable association. When you take out Penembic citizenship, perhaps you would care—"

"Soliciting a new member already, eh, Vegh?" said

the tall, thin grandee with the pointed gray beard. "Not sporting, you know."

"First come, first served," said Vegh.

"Excuse me, my lords," said Jorian. "I be not up on Irazi politics. Explain, pray."

Vegh smiled. "This is Lord Amazluek, stasiarch of the Kilts. Naturally, he would prefer to enlist you in his—"

"Bah!" said Amazluek. "The poor fellow has but lately arrived in Iraz. How should he know the glories of our ancient traditions, which my association cherishes and upholds? Be advised, young sir, that if you would fain make your way amongst people of the better sort here, you ought to abandon those barbarous nether garments—"

"I believe I was conversing with Master Jorian, when you cut in, Amazluek," said Vegh. "Will you kindly mind your business, whilst I—"

"It is my business!" cried Amazluek. "When I see three cozening an innocent young foreigner—"

"Cozening!" shouted Vegh. "Why, thou—"

"Gentlemen! Gentlemen!" said several courtiers, thrusting themselves between the angry stasiarchs.

"Anyway," said Amazluek, "none of *my* association has turned traitor and fled to the provinces to raise a rebellion!" He turned his back and stalked off.

"What he talk about?" said Jorian, looking innocent.

Vegh: "Oh, he alludes to that rascal Mazsan, leader of a dissident faction. He was a member of my honorable association ere we expelled him. There are always bloodthirsty extremists, and Mazsan is ours."

"Yes?"

"You see, Master Jorian, we—the Pants, that is— are the moderates of Iraz. We follow the middle way, in urging that the Royal Council be elected and given legislative powers. On one hand we have mossbacked conservatives, like Amazluek, who would hold back all progress. On the other, we have fanatics like Mazsan, who would abolish the monarchy altogether. We are the only sensible folk."

"What this about Mazsan disappearing?"

"He and some followers have dropped out of sight, and rumor says they fled the city when their attempt to unseat me failed. But none has seen them since. I suspect that some of Amazluek's rich young thugs caught the lot at a conspiratorial meeting, murdered them, and concocted the tale of their flight to discredit all the Pants. When—"

"Gentlemen!" wheezed the king. "We do believe we have seen enough for the nonce. Let us all return to the courtyard, where we shall have somewhat to say."

When they were drawn up in the courtyard in the middle of a hollow square of the Royal Guard, King Ishbahar said:

"It is our pleasure to announce that, in recognition of their services to our crown and state in repairing the clocks of the Tower of Kumashar, we hereby appoint Doctor Karadur of Mulvan director of the House of Learning, and Master Jorian of Kortoli our new clock-master. In recognition of their many years of faithful service, Doctor Borai and Clockmaster Yiyim are retired on pension. Doctor Borai is hereby made honorary commissioner of city planning."

"*Oi!* Who said I wanted to be clockmaster?" Jorian whispered to Karadur.

"Do be quiet, my son. You needs must do something whilst I grapple with the problem of your wife, and the pay is fair."

"Oh, well. Borai doesn't seem to like being pensioned."

"That is not surprising, seeing that his income will be halved. The city-planning thing carries no salary."

"Then we have another enemy to watch out for."

"You are too suspicious—"

"And now, gentlemen," said the king, "we shall return to our humble home. Doctor Karadur and Master Jorian, it is our pleasure that you take lunch with us this noon."

On the way from the tower to the palace, Jorian and Karadur passed through a huge gate in the wall surrounding the palace grounds. From the top of the gate rose a row of iron spikes, one of which bore a human head.

"The Gate of Happiness," said Karadur.

"That wight up yonder doesn't look very happy," said Jorian, indicating the head.

"Oh, this is the traditional place where heads of malefactors are exhibited."

"A curious conceit, to attach such a name to such a place."

"You utter verities, my son. The present monarch, howsomever, is mild and merciful, so that there is seldom more than one head on exhibition at a time. The conservatives grumble that such lenity encourages evildoers."

In the palace, the gentleman litter-bearers were dismissed by the king. Jorian and Karadur were conducted to a private dining room, where they ate with the king, alone but for a pair of guardsmen standing in the corners, a secretary who scribbled notes, and the king's food taster.

After amenities, Jorian brought up his brush with the pirates of Algarth on his voyage south. "From what I hear," he said, "they wax ever more aggressive along these coasts. I daresay Your Majesty knows what actions to take against them."

Looking unhappy, King Ishbahar spoke to the secretary: "Remind me to pass the word to Admiral Kyar, O Herekit." Then to Jorian: "Ah, that we could persuade these rogues to earn honest livings, like other men! Do you know that the ungrateful knaves have had the insolence to demand an increase in our annual largesse?"

"Means Your Majesty that you pay them trib—*unh*!" Jorian broke off as Karadur kicked his shin beneath the table. "I mean—ah—that your government subsidizes these gentry?"

"One might put it thus. One might. I know there is an argument for a hard policy; we have gone over it many a time and oft in council meetings. But our great philosopher Rebbim held that such men should not be blamed for their acts. The Algarthian Archipelago is a congeries of barren, sea-beaten rocks, where little food can be raised. The folk of that grim land must, therefore, resort to piracy or face starvation. So a subsidy, in return for immunity to our ships, seemed but a humane and benevolent act.

"Besides which, the subsidy was at first but a fraction of the cost of putting our navy on a war footing. Know you that the stroke man of a bench of rowers now gets three coppers a day? Some people are never satisfied." The king shook his head, his jowls wobbling. "But let us to a pleasanter subject. Do try this rhinoceros liver with sauce of lamprey's brains. You will swear that you have tasted nought like it, heh heh."

Jorian tried it. "Your Majesty is right," he said, swallowing manfully. "Your servant has never tasted aught like it. But, whilst Your Majesty's wish is my command, I have come to point where I can still chew but not swallow. I am full."

"Oh, come! A big, lusty swain like you? What you have eaten would not keep a bird alive. Not a bird."

"That depends upon the kind of bird, sire. I have already eaten thrice my usual lunch. Is like story of King Fusinian and the Teeth of Grimnor, which I told you."

The king's jowls quivered with laughter. "Ah, Master Jorian! Would that, had the gods permitted us children, we had a son like you!"

Startled, Jorian looked up. "Your Majesty's flattery overwhelms me. But..." he raised an inquiring eyebrow.

Karadur said: "Master Jorian is new to Iraz, sire, and he has been working night and day on the clocks. He is therefore unfamiliar with your dynastic situation."

"Our dynastic situation, as the learned doctor delicately puts it, is simple. We have had several wives, of whom two survive; but with all of these available females, we have begotten but one child, who died in infancy. So now we face the prospect of passing our crown on to one of a pair of worthless nephews.

"But let us speak of more cheerful things. In three

days comes the feast of Ughroluk, with the major races of the year. You two learned gentlemen shall occupy reserved seats in the Hippodrome, directly below the royal box. You will be safer there in case the factionists make a disturbance."

The king sighed as he looked at the still heaped plates before him. "Would we could spend the afternoon enjoying the harmless delights of the palate and interfering with none. But, alas, we must depart for our nap, after which we have a tedious matter of a lawsuit to decide. Ah, the rues of royalty!

"Know, Master Jorian, that in our youth we were deemed a bit of a scholar. In the libraries, you will still find our treatise on the pronunciation of Penembic in the days of Juktar the Great. But all that, alas, is far behind us. For the past year, we have endeavored to write our memoirs, but so implacably does public business nibble at our time that we have not yet reached the third chapter."

"I can sympathize," said Jorian. "I, too, have sometimes wished that I could have been a scholar, as Doctor Karadur is, in sooth. I did once study briefly at the Academy of Othomas; but the exigencies and contingencies of life have never let me abide in any one place long enough to get my teeth into a program of serious study."

"Now that you are living amongst us," said the king, "we are sure that this difficulty can be overcome. And now we must away once more. Fare you well, our friends."

Later, Jorian said: "He seems like an amiable old duck."

"Amiable, yes," said Karadur. "But he neglects public business to pamper his stomach, and he has no more spine than a bowlful of jelly. From a strictly moral point of view, I applaud his pacific outlook; but I fear it is impractical in this wicked world."

Jorian grinned. "You're the one who was always twitting me on my juvenile cynicism, as you called it, and now 'tis you who voice acerb views."

"I have probably caught some of your acrimonious outlook, like a contagious tisic. So long as the kingdom ride on an even keel, King Ishbahar may do well enough. But if a crisis arise—well, we shall see."

"Is this fellow Mazsan likely to overthrow him? So feeble a rule impresses me not as perdurable."

"Mazsan has dwelt in Novaria and returned full of lofty ideas for setting up a republic on the lines of Vindium. His following is formidable, since oppression and corruption are rife amongst Ishbahar's officials. Let us hope Mazsan never succeeds."

"Why so? The Vindines seem to do as well as the folk of any of the Twelve Cities, and things do not look good to me here."

"It is not Mazsan's ideas, which are not bad as such things go; it is the man himself. I know him. He is brilliant, energetic, and idealistic—but a hater, boiling with rancor and ferity. He has boasted that, when he attains power, there shall be displayed at the Gate of Happiness not one head but a thousand. There is a tale that he would even summon the wild nomads of Fedirun to help him to his goal."

"'Tis too bad that we cannot somehow sunder the man from his ideas," said Jorian.

"Aye; but that is the rock whereon many noble political schemes have gone to wrack. Mazsan could proclaim the world's most enlightened constitution, but that would do the Irazis no good when he began decapitating them by the hundred, as he would the instant he had power."

"So then," said Jorian, "the choice between that kindly mass of wobbling royal jelly and the gifted but bloodthirsty Master Mazsan is like the choice between being hanged and beheaded."

"True, but that is the way of the world."

V

THE
TUNNEL OF HOSHCHA

THE MORNING OF THE TWENTY-SIXTH WAS OVERCAST, presaging another autumnal rain. The mouth of the Lyap was covered with small craft, plying back and forth like a swarm of water insects as they conveyed thousands of Irazis across the river to Zaktan.

Jorian and Karadur strolled up the street that led from the Zaktanian waterfront. The street ended at the edge of the temenos of the temple of Nubalyaga. Following the flow of the crowd, Jorian and Karadur proceeded around the temple grounds to the right. This brought them to the temple entrance at the eastern end of the temenos.

The temple was a huge structure of domes and spires. The silver plating of its tiles glowed softly under the gray sky. Flanking the entrance were two thirty-foot statues of Nubalyaga in the form of a beautiful naked woman. One statue showed her as bending a huge bow; the other, pouring water from a jar.

"The one on the left is chasing away the eclipse," said Karadur, "whilst the other controls the tides."

Jorian stopped to look. "That's funny," he said. "Last night I dreamt that a woman just like that sculptor's model appeared unto me."

"Oh? What did she?"

"She said something like: 'Beware the second crown, my son.' Since the dame was clad as you see those statues, and since I have been unwontedly virtuous since you and I parted in Metouro, I sought to make love to her; but she turned to smoke and vanished. Since I thought the dream but a manifestation of my bridled lusts, and since the words did not seem to make sense, I paid no special heed and have now forgotten the rest of the vision."

"Hm. One needs must be alert to such things, because the gods—ah—really do appear to mortals thus, as you well know."

"If the advice of this goddess be no better than that of that little green god, Tvasha, who advised us in Shven, I can do without it."

Since the temple stood on an elevation, the street leading eastwards from it sloped downwards. Down this street flowed a river of folk: Irazis, the men in kilts or trousers and their women in enveloping robes; foreigners from Fedirun and Novaria and even—sweating in their furs and heavy woolens—blond barbarians from distant Shven. Among the Irazi men, kilt-wearing partisans sported the red and white colors of their faction, while adherents of the Pants wore blue and gold.

"It gratifies me to hear that you are subduing the lusts of the flesh," said Karadur. "It is the requisite preliminary step towards moral perfection and spiritual enlightenment. Have you, then, adhered to some ascetic philosophy or cultus?"

"Nay; I merely felt that Estrildis would mislike it if she knew I'd been dipping my wick. That's love for you. If I ever get her back, I'll make up for lost time."

They came to the outer wall of the Hippodrome, where rows of stone arches, one atop another, supported the tiers of seats. The crowd divided and flowed around the structure to the entrances. Jorian said:

"Our passes admit us through Entrance Four. Which is that?"

"To the right," replied Karadur.

Hawkers of flags, toy chariots, handwritten programs, and food and drink mingled with the crowd, crying their wares. Jorian and Karadur found Entrance Four and were swept in with the tide. An usher saluted as he saw the royal passes and directed their holders to seats below the royal box, at the halfway mark on one side of the long, elliptical course.

Jorian and Karadur settled in their seats and opened their lunch. On their left, where seats were reserved for active members of the Pants, the stands were a mass of blue and gold. On their right, red and white likewise filled the stands in the bloc composed of Kilts. Members of the two blocs scowled at each other across the intervening strip reserved for noblemen and officials, where sat Jorian and Karadur. Now and then, an epithet was shouted above the general din.

Jorian was finishing his beer when a fanfare announced the king. All in the stands arose as Ishbahar waddled into his box and lowered himself into the gilded throne. When the audience had sat again, the king motioned to his crier, who produced a speaking trumpet. The king held up a sheet of reed paper and a reading glass. He began to read in his wheezy squeak, pausing between sentences so that the crier could bellow his words.

It was a dull little speech, what Jorian could understand of it: "...auspicious occasion...glorious nation...gallant contestants...good sportsmanship...may the best team win..."

As the king finished, a man arose from among the Pants and shouted: "When will Your Majesty bring the slayers of Sefer to book?"

The king replied through his crier: "Pray, good sir, do not bring up this question now. The time is inappropriate. We are pursuing the matter..." But the voice even of the leather-lunged crier was lost in the chant of "Justice! Justice!" that rose from the massed Pants. In their turn, the Kilts began shouting in rhythm: "Down! Quiet! Down! Quiet!"

"Who's Sefer?" asked Jorian.

"An official of the Pants, who was found slain. The Pants swear he was killed by a gang of Kilts; the Kilts deny all knowledge of it."

The shouts of the crier, together with a threatening move on the part of the squads of gleaming guardsmen in bronzen cuirasses and crested steel helmets, at length abated the shouts of the rival factionists.

71

"They are putting the tortoise race first," said Karadur, "to amuse the mob and take the factionists' minds—if that be the word I wish—off their feud."

At the starting post at one end of the course, Jorian sighted through his spyglass four huge tortoises. When they stood up on their thick, bowed legs, the tops of their shells were the height of a tall man from the ground. On the back of each tortoise was strapped a saddle, similar to a camel saddle. On each saddle sat a man in motley clown's costume.

At the blast of a trumpet, the four tortoises ambled forward. It took them a long time to reach the part of the track directly before Jorian. In the meantime, bets flew thick and fast.

As the tortoises plodded past at a slow walk, the crowd roared at the antics of the riders, of whom two wore the colors of the Kilts and two, those of the Pants. They reached out to thwack one another with slapsticks, turned somersaults off their mounts and bounded back on, and indulged in a hundred zany gambols.

Jorian: "I feel a certain kinship for the Kilts, even though I wear trews."

"How so, my son? Are you becoming aristocratical-minded?"

"Not at all. Their colors, red and white, are those of the flag of Xylar. The Xylarian war cry, in fact, was 'red and white!'" Jorian sighed. "Betimes I regret that those lackwits wouldn't let me show what a good king I could be."

The tortoises passed on around to the other side of the course. A single circuit constituted their race. The good humor of the crowd seemed to have been restored.

Next came a race between two teams of zebras. Then a detachment of the Royal Guard, their metal polished to mirrorlike surfaces, marched around the course to the tune of a military band, stopping from time to time to perform a brief precision drill with their spears.

Six camels, ridden by brown-robed Fediruni desert men, raced four laps around the course. Then a float bearing a gilded image of the god Ughroluk, drawn by white oxen and preceded by a hundred priests singing a mighty hymn, passed slowly around the course. Many in the crowd joined the priests in singing. The god, crowned with ostrich plumes dyed scarlet and gold and emerald, bore a silver thunderbolt in one hand and a golden sunbeam in the other.

A pair of King Ishbahar's elephants, draped in purple and gold, lumbered around the track, not seeming to hurry much despite the yells of their mahouts and the whacks of their goads. Then two teams of unicorns raced.

"Now come the horses," said Karadur. "Being the fleetest draft animals, their race will decide the day as between the Pants and the Kilts."

Tension grew. A trumpet peal sent the four teams off. As the four chariots—two blue and gold, two crimson and silver—thundered past, the roar from the blocks of factionists drowned out all other sounds.

There were seven laps to the race. With each lap, the excitement waxed. As the chariots whirled past, men stood up, shaking fists, sobbing, frothing, and screaming.

When the cluster of vehicles rounded the first turn on the fourth lap, there was a crash and a glimpse of pieces of chariot flying. Two cars had collided. A detached wheel continued along the course on its own for half a bowshot before toppling over. When the dust had blown away enough for Jorian to see, he glimpsed a pair of stretcher-bearers trotting across the sand to pick up a victim. There was also a glimpse of an injured horse struggling to rise.

By the time the two surviving cars approached on their next lap, the service crew had largely cleared away the wreckage. The two survivors passed and repassed on the straightaway, neither able to gain a definitive advantage. On the last lap, they whirled to the finish line abreast. As they sped past the royal box, Jorian could not see that either had the advantage.

Officials huddled in consultation at the edge of the track. Then a pair of them hastened up the steps to the royal box. More consultation, and the crier shouted:

"Driver Paltoi, of the Pants, wins!"

The Pants applauded. Jorian noted that the Penembians applauded like Novarians, by clapping their hands, not by snapping their fingers like Mulvanians.

A growl arose from the Kilts. It grew, mingled with cries of "Foul! Foul!" The Pants shouted back.

"Was there a foul?" asked Jorian.

Karadur shrugged. "Alas, I am no expert on sports; nor are my old eyes up to detecting such irregularities. Natheless, methinks we had better make ourselves scarce."

"Why?"

"The races are over, all but the awards to the winners; but my spiritual senses tell me a riot is brewing. Besides, it looks like rain."

"All right," said Jorian, rising.

As he did so, a large beer mug, turning over and over in the air, flew from the bloc of Kilts towards the Pants. It struck Jorian's head with a crash and shattered. Jorian slumped back into his seat.

"My boy!" cried Karadur. "Are you injured?"

Jorian shook his head. "That does not seem to have split what few brains I have left. Let's go."

He rose again, staggering a little, and started for the exit. A trickle of blood ran down one side of his face.

More missiles flew over the central strip between the two blocs of factionists. As the gentry in this strip left their seats to run for cover, the two blocs rose and rushed at each other, drawing hitherto hidden daggers and short swords. Trumpets blew. The crier screamed. Whistles sounded.

Squads of glittering guardsmen clattered hither and yon, striving to beat the combatants apart with spear shafts. Others fought their way to the royal box to protect the king, who sat quivering and helplessly waving his fat hands. Fighting spread all over the Hippodrome, while the more peaceable members of the audience ran for the exits. The noise grew deafening.

Pulling Karadur by one bony wrist, Jorian forced his way through the crush at Entrance Four. In the concourse outside, knots of factionists were already hurling missiles, brandishing improvised clubs, kicking, punching, and stabbing.

Jorian tried to thread his way among the combatants to the main entrance without becoming embroiled. As he reached the gate, a fierce yell from behind made him turn.

"Kill the dirty foreigners!" shrieked a man. A flash of lightning revealed the man as Borai, the former director of the House of Learning. He was haranguing a group of armed Kilts. Beside him stood Yiyim, the former clockmaster. Thunder growled.

"The old witch cast a spell on our team!" screamed Borai. "That cost us our victory!"

"And the young one is his apprentice!" added Yiyim. "Slay them both! Tear them to pieces!"

The well-gnawed carcass of a chicken whirled through the air and missed Jorian; so did a horse turd. A paving stone, however, grazed Jorian's already bloody scalp and staggered him.

"Run, my son!" gasped Karadur.

"Whither?" shouted Jorian.

"The temple! To the temple of Nubalyaga! Demand sanctuary!"

The pair trotted across the street, just as rain began to fall. The gang of Kilts broke into a run behind them. As they reached the slope leading up to the temple, Karadur said:

"Go on, my son. I cannot run up yon hill."

"I won't leave you—"

"Go on, I say! I am old; you have many years—"

Without further words, Jorian gathered up the ancient bag of bones in his arms and ran up the hill carrying Karadur, despite the Mulvanian's pleas. Jorian slipped on the rain-wet cobblestones and fell; Karadur's bulbous turban came off and rolled away. Jorian scrambled up again with his burden and ran on. The mob behind them gained.

At the entrance to the temple, a pair of eunuch guards, standing inside the gate, crossed their spears to bar the way. Jorian, his red face streaked with mingled rain,

sweat, mud, and blood, was too winded to speak. Karadur
cried:

"Admit us in the name of the lady Sahmet, sirs! I
am Doctor Karadur of the House of Learning!"

The eunuchs lowered their spears. As soon as Jorian
and Karadur were inside, the eunuchs clanged the bronzen gate valves shut. Other guards hastened from other
parts of the temenos. In a trice, a dozen eunuchs, with
cocked crossbows, stood in a line behind the gate.

"Begone, or we will shoot through the bars!" they
shouted.

The mob milled and screamed but made no effort to
assault the gate. Jorian and Karadur hastened towards
the main temple building.

"I owe you my life," said Karadur.

"Oh, nonsense! Had I thought the matter out, I should
probably have left you. You almost deserve it for as-
suring me that Borai and Yiyim were harmless. Where's
this Lady Sahmet?"

"I will send in our names. If she be not engaged in
ritual, methinks she will see us."

Despite the drizzle, the mob of Kilts, under the lead-
ership of Borai and Yiyim, had spread out into a cordon,
which seemed to be extending itself clear around the
temenos.

"They're laying siege to the place," said Jorian.

"I am sure the king's men will clear them away. If
not, belike Sahmet can solve our difficulty."

"If we had one of those flying things you have spoken
of, we could flit over their heads. But then, if we had
a carriage, we should have a horse and carriage, if we
had a horse. Isn't that a fire?" Jorian pointed to a column
of smoke and sparks, which rose above the nearby roofs.

"Aye; the fools will burn down the city if given a
free hand."

High Priestess Sahmet received Jorian and Karadur
in her chamber of audience. She was a tall, large-boned
woman in her forties, handsome but too massive of jaw
and beaklike of nose to be called beautiful. Clad in a
gauzy robe of pale gray embroidered with symbols in

76

silver thread, she sat in a chair of pretence and stared with large, dark eyes at the disheveled fugitives. A couple of lesser priestesses glided about.

"It is a pleasure to see you again, good Doctor Karadur," she said in a deep, resonant voice, "albeit one could wish the circumstances less frantic. And who is the young man?"

"I am Jorian the Kortolian," said Jorian, "presently clockmaster to His Majesty. I am honored to meet Your Sanctity."

The woman gave Jorian a penetrating stare. She snapped her fingers. "Inkyara! More light, if you please." When a branched candlestick had been set on a taboret and lit, Sahmet said:

"Master Jorian, methought I knew you."

"Madam! I misdoubt I have had the pleasure—"

"I mean not in the sense of knowing you on this material plane. But I have seen you in visions."

"Yes, madam?"

"You are the barbarian savior!"

"Eh? Oh, come now, Madam Sahmet. I am no barbarian! I learnt my letters when I was but five, in school in Ardamai; and I have studied at the Academy at Othomae. My table manners may not be up to courtly standards, but I do not make a pig of myself. I am only an honest craftsman, and in any case I am unqualified to save Iraz from any doom. But what mean you to do with us?"

"Not cast you to that slavering mob, certes." She spoke in an undertone to one of the lesser priestesses, who glided out and presently returned. After a whispered colloquy, Sahmet said:

"Fires have sprung up in several parts of Iraz as well as Zaktan, and the soldiers are too busy fighting them to control the mobs of factionists. The crowd of Kilts surrounding this temple has been reinforced, so you cannot leave by the streets."

"Neither have we magical power to fly over their heads," said Jorian.

"Let me think," said Sahmet. "I am loath to harbor you overnight, since for entire males to pass the night here, other than on the occasion of the Divine Marriage, would offend the goddess. Happily, there is another course. Ere I reveal it to you, howsomever, I must have your promise to do me a small favor in return."

Jorian's eyes narrowed. "Madam, I have been in and out of not a few tight places in my short life, and buying pigs in pokes is one thing I have learnt to avoid. If I can, I shall be glad to help you—but I must needs know about this favor."

"It amounts to little. I do but ask that you play a small part in one of our forthcoming observances."

"If you mean to make a eunuch of me, madam—"

"Bountiful heavens, nothing like that! I solemnly promise that it shall cost you not the least scrap of your splendid physique. More I cannot say now."

"Nor senses, faculties, and abilities?"

"Nor those, either. Well, sir?"

Jorian argued a little more, but no further details could he elicit from Sahmet. He exchanged glances with Karadur, but the old wizard was not helpful. Jorian did not like to promise anything under such vague conditions, but he saw no alternative.

"Very well, Madam Sahmet," he said, "I agree."

"Good! You shall not rue your choice. Now come with me."

An assistant priestess hurried up with a small lanthorn, which she handed to Sahmet. The high priestess led them out. They passed through halls and rooms and down steps until Jorian was lost. In an underground passage, dimly lit by a single sconce, Sahmet halted at a massive, bolted, wooden door.

"Master Jorian," she said, "I would not do this for any wight, even to save life. But, since this peril involves the barbarian savior, I have no choice." She slipped a massive ring off one finger. "Take this. When you come to the door at the far end of the tunnel, knock four times, thus." She tapped twice with a knuckle, paused, and tapped twice more. "When the peephole opens, show this ring—which, may I add, I wish returned when this peril has passed."

She drew back the bolt and opened the door. Then

she held out a hand. "Fare you well, gentlemen." She gripped Jorian's hand longer and more forcibly than he expected. "I may see you again, Master Jorian—and sooner than you think."

She handed Jorian the lanthorn, whose single candle stub sent feeble rays through its windows of glass. The heavy door boomed shut behind Jorian and Karadur.

The passageway sloped down and down and down. The stones lining the tunnel became wet and slimy. Jorian said:

"This must be that tunnel under the Lyap I've heard of. I am sure we're below the water table."

"The what, my son?"

"The water table. Know you not how, a certain distance below the surface, water fills up all the pores betwixt the grains of soil? Hence, if one digs below that level, one gets a well."

"Nay, I did not know, having devoted my life to the spiritual as opposed to the material sciences. How learnt you such things?"

"I picked them up when I was surveying for the Syndicate of Ir."

"You are assuredly a versatile fellow."

Jorian grinned in the gloom. "I suppose I am." He recited:

"Oh, Jorian was a man of many parts;
    He'd gallop on a fiery steed of war,
    Cross swords with desperados, or
Purloin from maidens fair their gentle hearts;
Whip up a sonnet, rondeau, or sestine,
    Discharge a deadly shaft, repair a clock,
    Administer a kingdom, pick a lock,
Survey a road, or sail a barquentine.

"For all his many skills, this artful man
    Could never reach the goal for which he played,
    Which was to settle with a loving wife,
Become a quiet, bourgeois artisan,

And prosecute some worthy, peaceful trade
   Throughout a long and uneventful life."

Jorian hastened to add: "I'm really not so self-conceited as all that. 'Tis just that the rhyme amused me."

Karadur chuckled. "My boy, you are all that you say; albeit I doubt that you are really so determined upon a quiet life as you proclaim. Otherwise you would not—"

"Oh, yes? And who dragged me from my quiet, peaceful surveying job to this hotbed of intrigue and insurrection?"

"Ah, but in your last letter you said you would do aught to recover your Estrildis."

"Oh, well, so I did. But now I'm sure we are below the Lyap. What keeps the water out? I see no pumps."

"The water is kept from Hoshcha's Tunnel by a trio of wizards, spell-casting night and day. They are Goelnush, Luekuz, and Firaven, in my Department of Applied Thaumaturgy. Just now the House of Learning is embroiled in a furious feud, which I am supposed to resolve and compose. So high has partisan feeling run that the deans of my two schools will not speak to each other."

"What's this?"

"Goelnush, Luekuz, and Firaven form part of the School of Spirit. Now, engineers in the School of Matter claim that with pumps of the latest design, they can keep the tunnel as dry as my three wonder-workers, at less cost and with less chance of failure. The dean of the School of Spirit retorts that pumps are quite as likely to break down as a group of well-trained thaumaturges; that besides labor to furnish power for the pumps, we should require plumbers to keep the pumps and pipes in order; and that the pumping apparatus with its pipes would occupy so much of the tunnel that it would impede the king's monthly journeys through it."

"Is this the Divine Marriage whereof Zerlik told me?"

"Aye. You know of that, then?"

"I know what Zerlik told me. Is this ritual marriage consummated?"

"Well—ah—yes, it is. In sooth, when the king can no longer play his manful part, he is disposed of."

"Good gods, this is as bad as Xylar! How is it done?"

"When the king can no longer—ah—carnally penetrate the high priestess, she reports the fact to her nominal husband, the high priest of Ughroluk. Then the high priest, with a delegation of lesser priests, waits upon the king and presents him with the sacred rope, wherewith to hang himself."

"And the silly ass does it?"

"Aye; although this suicide has taken place but once in the last century. All the other kings have perished in war, or by assassination, or from some common ill, ere the rope came into play."

Holding his lanthorn up, Jorian walked a few steps along the dark tunnel in silence. Then he said:

"By Thio's horns, you don't suppose that promise Sahmet exacted from me was to take the king's place in this ceremony?"

"I know not, my son, but I fear she had some such scheme in mind."

"There you are! I listen to your moral preachments on the virtues of continence and try to practise them; but the very gods conspire against my new-found virtue."

"True, O Jorian. Little though I esteem fornication, I fear I must condone it this once."

"Well, that's something. At least, I don't suppose Sahmet will turn into a gigantic serpent, as did the princess Yargali. Now, I can see why Sahmet might not find Ishbahar to her taste as a bedfellow. But why pick on me?"

"You were to hand; she has seen you—or claims she has seen you—in her visions; and perhaps she finds you attractive."

"If I'm attractive to her looking like this, she'll find me utterly ravishing when cleaned up. Well, I daresay I can hold up my end, in all senses of the phrase. We won't tell Estrildis about it and hope that, if she find out, she'll forgive me natheless."

"Your secret is safe with me, my son."

81

"Good. But why need the king anything so costly as this tunnel for his connubial visits? Why cannot he cross the Lyap in a boat, like everyone else?"

Karadur shrugged. "Some say that King Hoshcha—who was not of the line of Juktar the Great and whose right to the throne was therefore questioned—was full of fancies about being assassinated as he rode through the streets. Others aver that he wished the tunnel as a means of escape from his palace in the event of revolution. In any case, he began the use of the tunnel for the Divine Marriage, and his successors have imitated him."

"What finally happened to Hoshcha?"

"After all his precautions—which included wearing a steel breastplate under his robes—he slipped in getting out of his bath and fractured his skull."

At the head of the long, narrow flight of steps that ended Hoshcha's Tunnel, Jorian rapped four times on the heavy door. When the peephole opened, he held up Sahmet's ring.

A bolt clanked and the door groaned open. There stood King Ishbahar in a dressing gown, without his wig. The lamplight shone on his egg-bald pate. A pair of guardsmen stood behind him; beyond these, servants hovered.

"By Nubalyaga's cleft!" cried the king. "Jorian! Whatever befell you, my boy? Come in, come in! You, too, Doctor."

They stepped into the king's dressing room, and Jorian told briefly what had happened to him and his companion since the start of the riot. A guardsman closed the door, which became merely one more panel in the wall. The handle of the bolt that secured it looked like a piece of gilded ornamentation.

"You did the proper thing," said the king. "We shall order the arrest of those villains Borai and Yiyim. You two shall sup with us this even. But first, my dear Jorian, you must clean up. You look as if you had been fighting a dragon and getting the worst of it, heh heh. You shall have the use of our royal bathtub, no less!"

"Your Majesty's consideration overwhelms me," said Jorian.

"Stuff and nonsense, my boy! We are friends, not merely sovran and subject. Evvelik! Conduct these gentlemen to the bathroom and furnish them with the needfuls."

The royal bathtub was a huge affair of burnished copper. As Jorian soaked and soaped, he murmured to Karadur, who was washing his face and hands:

"O Karadur, is this king deemed a little queer?"

"Nay; barring his fondness for the table—"

"I mean, with a lust for boys or men in lieu of women."

"Oh, ah I see. Nay again. Whereas that aberration is rife in Irazi, I think not that the charge has ever been laid against Ishbahar. When young, he had several wives, of whom all but two have died or been cast off; but I know of no other outlet for his lusts. Forsooth, methinks his only present passion is for rare victuals. Why?"

"Why else should he seek to make a bosom friend and confidant of a nobody—a mere foreign artisan— like me? It makes no sense."

"Perchance he simply likes you, my son. Or again, perchance it is concerned with Sahmet's plans for you."

"Oh. We must look further into this matter. And by the bye, meseems this tub were an admirable flying vehicle for our foray into Xylar. If we kept the weight well down in it, 'twere stabler than the common flying carpet or broomstick."

Karadur shook his head dubiously. "It would take a mighty demon to loft such a weight, and demons resist being imprisoned in copper or silver, since they know it is difficult for them to escape therefrom."

"Why not try Gorax, whom you keep mewed up in that ring? He's the strongest demon I know of."

"Alas, Gorax owes me but one more labor. Then he will be free to return to his own plane. Hence I dare not release him save for the direst need."

"I should have thought that being chased by that mob this afternoon were a case of direst need."

"True; but so scattered were my old wits that I never thought of Gorax at all."

Over one of King Ishbahar's colossal repasts, Jorian asked: "How went the riots, Your Majesty?"

"Luckily for Iraz, the rain waxed so heavy that it dispersed the factionists. Hence only a few score were slain and a few houses looted and burnt. This factiousness is a dreadful thing, but we know not how to end it. Have some of these oysters, which have come all the way from the coast of Shven, packed in ice."

"Why not simply stop the races, sire?"

"Ah, one of our predecessors—Huirpalam the Second, as we recall—tried that. Then the two factions united to revolt, drag poor Huirpalam to the Hippodrome, and tear him to pieces—a small piece at a time. We would not invite a similar fate, heh heh."

"If you will pardon your servant's saying so, methinks Your Majesty will have to face these factions down, soon or late. But that is Your Majesty's concern. Tell me, sire, what is this about Madam Sahmet's wishing me to take part in a service to the moon goddess?"

The king looked startled. "She has told you already? One moment." He sighed to everybody present save Jorian and Karadur—even the bodyguards and the food taster—to leave the chamber. Then he said, barely above a whisper: "Know you the fate of a futterless king in Penembei?"

"I have been told of it, sire."

"It is true." The king pointed to a massive bracket overhead, whence hung a lamp. "All too true. They take away that lamp, and we are supposed to toss the rope over yon gallows. We stand on a table, make fast the knot, and overset the table—ugh! Thus they get rid of an unwanted monarch without laying impious hands on his sacred person."

"Is Your Majesty finding his sacerdotal duties—ah—"

"Arduous? Have we your solemn oath of secrecy?"

Jorian and Karadur both swore. Ishbahar went on: "Our life is in your hands. We would not entrust it to you gentlemen, save that desperate conditions demand desperate remedies. For several months, now, our lady Sahmet has been dissatisfied with our performance; and forsooth, we had as lief abandon such games, since our girth imposes mechanical difficulties upon the coital process, and the fires of youth have long since burnt low.

"So, you see, our life is already in the hands of Madam Sahmet. She has but to tell her nominal husband, High Priest Chaluish, and he will pay us a visit with the sacred rope. She refrains for two reasons: Imprimus, that she hates High Priest Chaluish and would do nought to favor him; secundus, that I have promised her a lusty springald with an iron yard as my surrogate, an she will keep tacit about my limitations. And you shall be he."

Jorian: "I trust I shall prove worthy of the honor. But we once had a king in Kortoli who faced a similar predicament."

"Tell us, dear boy."

"This was King Finjanius, who reigned just after the Dark Age following the fall of Old Novaria to nomadic invaders from Shven. The Kortolian rule was that, when the king was no longer for any reason deemed worthy to rule, the chief priests of the kingdom called upon him to present him with a goblet of poison to drink. If he drank not, they said, the magical nexus betwixt him and his land would be broken, and the crops would wither and the people starve.

"Now, Finjanius was sent to the Academy at Othomae for his higher education. The Academy was then a new institution with but a handful of professors— none of the ivy-clad buildings it now boasts. In the Academy, Finjanius absorbed what were then deemed heretical 'modern' ideas. Shortly after his return from Othomae, he succeeded to the throne when his uncle, the old king, died.

"For a year or so, Finjanius ran the affairs of Kortoli according to his best lights. Being young, he had little reverence for tradition and introduced many novelties, such as no longer requiring subjects to knock their heads on the ground nine times in approaching him, or no longer forbidding them to speak to him unless he spoke first. This last rule had nearly lost him a military campaign against Aussar, when none of his officers durst warn him of an ambush.

"Finjanius it was who introduced the public bath to Kortoli and encouraged all the people, regardless of age, sex, or rank, to mingle freely in these establishments. Moreover, he patronized them himself and did not scruple to indulge in vulgar horseplay with his subjects, splashing and ducking them and being splashed and ducked in turn.

"Such conduct made him popular with the commons but gravely offended the more conservative elements. These at length determined that Finjanius needs must go. Since the chief priests also belonged to the leading and most tradition-bound families, a concensus was soon obtained. Presently, a delegation of priests waited upon the king with the fatal draft.

"'Oho!' quotha. 'what is this?'

"'The gods,' said the high priest of Zevatas, 'have decided that Your Majesty is no longer worthy to rule.'

"'How know you that, sirrah?' said Finjanius.

"'They have informed us in visions and dreams, sire,' replied the priest. 'They demand the life of the chiefest man of the kingdom, lest they loose their wrath upon the land.'

"'So they crave the chiefest life, eh?' said the king. He counted the priests and found that there were eight in the party. 'Now, whereas I am doubtless the chief man in Kortoli, you holy fathers are also not without standing. Would you not agree, messires?'

"'Aye, sire; else we were not qualified to pass the gods' commands on to you.'

"'In sooth, let us suppose that the life of one of you is worth—ah—let us say, one eighth of mine. That were plausible, were it not?'

"'Aye, milord king,' said the priest.

"'Then,' said Finjanius, 'an the gods desire the chiefest life, they should be just as well satisfied with eight lives, each worth one eighth of mine. Ho, guards! Seize me these eight gentlemen and hang them forthwith!'

"And so it was done. Thereafter none durst broach such a proposal to the king again, and hence the custom fell into abeyance."

King Ishbahar said: "Do you propose, dear Jorian, that we adopt a course like unto your king's?"

"That is up to Your Majesty. It has been done; and what men have done, men can do again." Jorian turned to Karadur. "Is that not one of the proverbs of your Mulvanian sage, what is his name?"

"Cidam," said Karadur.

The king shuddered, his chins quivering. "Alas! Would—would that we had the hardihood to essay such an enterprise." A pair of tears trickled down his fat cheeks. "But we *could* not defy tradition. We fear we are not of the stuff of your Finjanius." The king burst into sobs and covered his face with his hands.

"Your Majesty!" said Karadur. "An your servitors and guardsmen return and find you weeping, they will think we have entreated you ill and slay us."

The king wiped his face with his napkin and smiled through his tears. "Let us forget our griefs, then. Have some more of this Vindine wine! Master Jorian, we trust you are an entire man, with the usual lusts and faculties?"

"Aye, sire."

"Then you should not find the task confronting you arduous or disagreeable. Whilst a trifle older than you, Sahmet is neither unattractive nor cold. Neither. Remember, it is not just your prick that you pleasure, but our royal neck, as well, that you save. We will have Herekit make you out a commission as Friend of the King forthwith, for such you will be in a most literal way."

"I thank Your Majesty," said Jorian. "When does this sacred orgy take place?"

"At the next full moon, eleven nights hence. Let us drink to your success. May you give Her Sanctity a night she shall remember to her grave!"

VI

THE GOLEM GENERAL

NEXT MORNING, JORIAN WENT TO THE TOWER OF KUmashar to inspect his clocks. He was pleased to find that yesterday's disturbances had not reached the tower. Then he made his way through the bustling crowds to the House of Learning.

Knowing him by now, the sentries admitted him without question. As he walked through the halls, he lingered at the doors of several laboratories where experiments were in progress. In one, engineers of the School of Matter tinkered with a machine designed to run on the power from boiling water. The project was old, but none had yet succeeded in making the contraption do any useful work. In another, technicians worked on a telescope, like the ordinary spyglass but much larger, wherewith they hoped to investigate the heavenly bodies.

Other chambers were in use by wizards of the School of Spirit. In one, three such sages sought to train a demon from the tenth plane, a creature of low intelligence, to obey simple commands. In another, a wizard-physician experimented with a spell to cure plague; his subjects were condemned criminals who had volunteered for the task on the promise of freedom if they survived.

Besides these activities, many rooms stood empty. As a result of the decline of the kings' financial support of the House of Learning, the size of its personnel and the scale of its projects had greatly shrunk in recent decades.

"At least," said Jorian, seated in the director's office, "yesterday's misadventures finally led you to get a new turban. That old one was getting so decrepit that I expected to find mice nesting in it." He had had his own hair cut short to bandage the wounds on his scalp.

"Contemn not such old things, my son," said Karadur. "That turban had acquired some small magical potential, merely by being in the vicinity when so many fell incantations were uttered and spells were cast. Do your clocks run harmoniously?"

"As regularly as the heavenly bodies. I've just come from the Tower. There was never any real problem, had your predecessor hired a competent mechanic instead of a fumbler. My father did a good, workmanlike job, as anyone who knew him could have told you.

"What I've come for, howsomever, is not the state of the clocks but the state of Jorian of Ardamai. Have you a means for our raid into Xylar?"

"Gods of Mulvan, Jorian, be not so hasty! Here we have barely escaped with our lives from riot and insurrection; we have traversed the most secret passageway in the kingdom; we have become embroiled in the conflict amongst the king, Madam Sahmet, and High Priest Chaluish—"

"All the more reason for pressing on. What's Chaluish like?"

"A little gray-haired man—nobody whom one would look at twice. He was in that parade of priests yesterday, and I have encountered him at courtly functions. But—"

"I have the *Flying Fish* tied up in a private dock for a small monthly rental, but I fear she'd prove too slow if we really had to run for it. So we had better prepare some swifter magical vehicle—"

"My son, I have never said that I would accompany you on your mission of abduction. Much though I esteem the lady Estrildis, I cannot desert a responsible post for petty personal—"

"Petty!" barked Jorian. "I'll have you know—"

"Now, now, my son, I meant no offense. But you

have seen how this kingdom totters along, and I—unworthy though I be—am in a position to lend it a little stability and rationality. It were irresponsible—"

"I quote," growled Jorian: "'So convenient a thing it is to be a reasoning being, for it enables one to think up a plausible reason for whatever one wishes to do.'"

"The wise Cidam?"

"Nay; our home-grown Novarian philosopher Achaemo. But, my reverend old spooker, my task needs at least two persons."

"Take Zerlik," said Karadur. "The lad will be delighted."

"What, and have to wipe that idiot's nose at every step? No, thank you! He'd do something silly at the critical moment, such as challenging the captain of the guard to a duel just when I was trying to hoist Estrildis out undetected."

"At least, he is reasonably strong and agile. I am neither, nor am I any longer up to such desperate adventures. Another journey like ours around the Inner Sea would terminate this incarnation for me."

"You can still cast a dire spell, which Zerlik cannot. But let's leave the question of personnel for the nonce to discuss the vehicle. How about that royal copper bathtub?"

Karadur wagged his head. "Alas, I see no prospect of obtaining it for your purpose. Even supposing that I could persuade the king to lend it—"

"Build another like it, then."

"That were too costly. It would come to hundreds of royals, and I have no funds in this year's appropriation to cover it.

"Furthermore, you appear not to realize the practical difficulties. It would require months of the most puissant sorcery to entrap our demon and compel him to our will. For such an enterprise, my best men were Goelnush, Luekuz, and Firaven, but they are fully occupied with keeping Hoshcha's Tunnel dry. The other sorcerers at my command are all less competent. Old Oinash, for ensample, is but a doddery old timeserver awaiting his pension. Barch, a younger man, is gifted but careless. Twice he has barely escaped sudden death at the claws of a hostile demon he had evoked, through some silly error in his pentacle; but he never seems to learn. As for Yanmik—"

"Why not put these dimmer flames on the tunnel—which must now be mere routine—to release your best men for my spell?"

"The king has forbidden it. He is fain not to have the wizard on duty sneeze and let in the floods just as he is traversing the tunnel on his tryst with Sahmet. Therefore he insists that my best men be kept at this task. And speaking of the king, there is—ah—umm—another complication."

"What's this? Out with it!"

"The—ah—His Majesty but this morn forbade me to assist you in any way in leaving Iraz. He must be apprehensive as to what might befall him if you were not present at the next full moon to pleasure the priestess."

Jorian glowered. "Curse it, you hauled me away from a good, respectable job, where I was at least geographically near to my darling, to this distant and turbulent city, on the promise of getting me means to rescue her. All you needed, you said, was to become director of the House of Learning, and the fish was in the creel. Well, thanks to my clockery, you're now director—and what happens? You can't do this for this reason, and you can't do that for that, and so on. I can make things hot for people who betray me—"

"My son, my son! Pray, take not that harsh and hostile tone. At the moment, I admit I envisage no easy thoroughfare to your noble goal. Only have patience, and the gods will open the way for us. They have never met—yes, Nedef?" Karadur changed from Novarian to Penembic. "O Jorian, this is our official scryer; Master Nedef, I present Jorian the Kortolian, our new clockmaster. You were saying?"

"Doctor Karadur," said the scryer, "I fear I have portentous news."

"You may speak before Master Jorian."

"Iraz is threatened by a host of assailants."

"Eh? Vurnu, Kradha, and Ashaka! What assailants? We are at war with none."

"May I sit, sir? I am weak with what I have seen."

"By all means, sit. Now tell us forthwith."

The scryer drew a long breath. "North, east, south, and west—they converge upon us from all sides. From the west comes a fleet of Algarthian pirates; from the south, a rabble of armed peasants under Mazsan and his faction; from the east, a swarm of Fediruni nomads on camels; and from the north, a Free Company of mercenaries from Novaria."

"How nigh are they?"

"Some are nigher than others; they may reach us on the morrow."

"How got the Fedirunis past the army along our eastern borders? Have they defeated the frontier force?"

"I know not, Doctor. They were already well inside the border when I discovered them."

"We must notify the king instanter," said Karadur.

They found King Ishbahar at his afternoon repast, which he called "tea." "Sit down, sit down, our dear fellows!" he cried. "Have a cup of genuine tea, brought at vast expense from Kuramon in the Far East. Have some of these honey biscuits to go with it. Try some of these sardines. Have you tea in Novaria nowadays?"

"It can be obtained, Your Majesty," said Jorian, "but it has never really taken hold. Perhaps the fact that the upheavals in Salimor cut off the supply from time to time have discouraged its use. Howsomever—"

"The Novarians ought to take it up," said Ishbahar. "They are too much given to drunkenness, we hear. A pleasant but nonintoxicating drink were better for their health." The king bit off the end of a huge plantain from Beraoti. "Moderation in all things is our guiding principle. Temperance." The plantain rapidly diminished.

"No doubt, sire. But we have something important to—"

"In fact, dear boy, how would you like a royal conces-

92

sion, to freight tea up the coast to Xylar? You could build up a profitable trade—"

"Sire," said Jorian, "Iraz is about to be attacked. Had we not better break the impending siege ere discussing trade routes?"

"Iraz? Besieged?" said the king, holding an olive in front of his open mouth. "Nubalyaga save us, but what is this?"

Karadur explained the visions that the scryer had seen in his crystal ball.

"Oh, dear!" said the king, looking sadly at the piles of uneaten food. "To have to break off such a splendid tea in the middle! The sufferings we kings endure for the welfare of our people! Ho, Ebeji! Summon Colonel Chuivir!"

When the glittering commander of the Royal Guard had clanked in and saluted, Ishbahar asked Karadur to repeat his tale. Then he asked Chuivir:

"However did those barbarians get past the frontier undetected?"

"You forget, sire, that General Tereyai has assembled the frontier army for maneuvers in the foothills of the Lograms, leaving the border covered by only a skeleton force. The Fedirunis must have surprised one of the frontier fortresses and poured through ere the alarm could be spread."

"Where is Admiral Kyar?"

"I believe he has put to sea in his flagship, to exercise his rowers."

"Then, Colonel, you would seem to be the ranking officer in Iraz. Kindly get word to General Tereyai and Admiral Kyar as soon as you can. Meanwhile, you shall mobilize the Royal Guard and call up the companies of the factions."

"But, Your Majesty, how shall I—how do you wish me to carry out your commands? Shall I send a barge out to seek the admiral—"

Ishbahar slapped the table, making the cups and dishes dance. "Colonel Chuivir! Bother us not with those details; just carry out our orders! Now go and get to work!" When the crestfallen colonel had clanked out, the king shook his head. "Woe is us! We do believe we committed an error in appointing Chuivir to that command. He looked so magnificent on parade, but he has never fought a battle in his life."

"Then how did it happen, sire?" asked Jorian.

"He was a cousin of our third wife and well-liked in society. Since we relied upon the frontier force to keep the foe a decent distance from Iraz, we never expected that the actual defense of the city would devolve upon this amiable popinjay. Herekit!"

"Aye, sire?" said the secretary.

"Draft me a letter to Daunas, Grand Bastard of Othomae, inquiring whether he would hire out to us a few squadrons of his lobster-plated heavy cavalry, and on what terms. And command two of our swiftest couriers to stand by, booted and saddled. Draft another to Shaju, king of kings of Mulvan, urging him to invade the deserts of Fedirun from the east, since this land will be partly stripped of warriors. Suggest that he loot their sacred city of Ubar." The king turned back to his guests with a sigh. "Ah, well, we have done what we can. Now the fate of the city rests upon our gallant subjects."

"Does Your Majesty plan to take an active part in the defense?" asked Jorian.

"Bountiful heavens, dear boy, nay! Can you imagine us, with our girth, trading spear-thrusts on the battlements? Besides, we have always been a man of peace, with little use for fire-eating sword-rattlers. And now, meseems, our city and our life must needs depend upon these same swashbucklers. Doctor Karadur, you should muster your scientists and wizards to the work of defense. Have you, perchance, a spell to summon some unhuman race—say, the silvans of the Lograms—to our aid?"

"I will see what the House of Learning can do," said Karadur. "But let Your Majesty not count upon any such assistance. The unhumans have little love for mankind, having been harshly entreated by them. To seek to compel aid from them is like holding a sword by the wrong end, so that it wounds the hand of the wielder. But I go—"

"Stay, stay. Now that we have given the essential commands, there is no reason why we should not finish our tea."

"But, sire, I—"

"Nay, relax. A quarter-hour more or less will not decide the fate of the city. Do have some of these mushrooms, gathered in the jungles of Baraoti."

"If Your Majesty thinks them safe..." said Jorian, staring uneasily at a yellow-spotted purple fungoid growth of singularly repulsive appearance.

"Nonsense! We have been eating these for years, and we have not lost a royal taster yet, heh heh."

Jorian manfully swallowed a mouthful of fungus. To give himself a pretext for not eating another, he said:

"Your Colonel Chuivir reminds your servant of the tale of King Filoman and the golem general."

"Go ahead, dear boy," said the king. "You will not mind if we steal a bit of your mushroom, will you?"

"Feel free, sire."

"This king," began Jorian, "otherwise called Filoman the Well-Meaning, was the father of the celebrated Fusinian the Fox. King Filoman was also an outstanding ruler in his way. He had the noblest emotions and the best intentions of any Kortolian monarch. He was intelligent, courageous, honest, hard-working, moral, kind, and generous. His only fault was that he had no common sense, and in practice this fault often cancelled all his other virtues put together.

"One legend says that this fault was caused by an astrological conjunction at his birth. Another avers that, when the fairies gathered for his naming ceremony, the fairy who was supposed to confer common sense lost her temper when she beheld another fairy wearing a gauzy gown just like hers and flounced out in a rage without bestowing her gift.

"Early in his reign, King Filoman confronted the problem of the defense of his realm. Being a peace-loving man, he supposed that others felt likewise. In this opinion he was encouraged by his minister, an oldster named Periax whom he had inherited from the previous reign.

"Periax urged Filoman to reduce the army to a mere royal guard. 'Wars,' quotha, 'are caused by mutual fears and suspicions, which in turn are caused by armaments. Get rid of the armaments and you will abolish war. When our neighbors see us disarming, they will know that we have no aggressive intentions towards them and lose their fear of us. Then they will follow our example, and peace and brotherhood shall reign forevermore.'

"Periax did not enlarge upon the real reason for his advice. This was that he was himself too old and creaky to sit a horse, brandish a sword, and perform other warlike acts. In these early times, the king and his ministers were expected to lead charges in person. Periax reckoned that, as a result of his pacific policy, war would at least be deferred until after his natural death, and he cared not for what befell the kingdom thereafter.

"Periax's argument seemed to Filoman like sound sense, so he virtually disbanded his army. Now, at this time, Kortoli's southern neighbor, Vindium, was under the rule of Nevors the Daft, whose character is implied by his sobriquet. I need not detail the enormities of his reign: wasting his treasury on solid gold statues of himself; slaying ministers, kinsmen, and associates on the slightest pretext; whimseys like making his army dress up as frogs and go hopping about the parade ground on all fours, shouting *Diddit! Diddit!* while King Nevors rolled on the ground screaming with laughter.

"In time, a cabal of noblemen and officials got the king apart from his bodyguard, hacked him to pieces, and threw the pieces into the Inner Sea. Then the problem arose, who should take the unlamented Nevors' place? For he had slain all his near kin.

"As it happened, an astute and ambitious lawyer, Doctor Truentius, had foreseen these events and gathered a powerful following among the commons. When King Nevors was slain, Truentius marched to the palace at the head of thousands of his partisans, chased out the relicts of the old reign, and proclaimed a republic with himself as First Consul.

"Truentius was the most brilliant man in Vindium. He had read all the historians and philosophers and prophets and had thought deeply on questions of government. He it was who, more or less singlehanded, invented republican government in Novaria. He drew up a constitution for Vindium which, considering its early date, is still acclaimed as a marvel of profound and original thought.

"Knowing himself the ablest man around, Truentius inferred that his decisions as to what was best for the Vindines were necessarily right. Therefore, anyone who opposed them was by definition an enemy of the people and hence a scoundrel for whom the direst punishment were too lenient. Soon Vindium City saw in its main square a large wooden block, served by a man with a black hood over his head and a large ax in his hands, wherewith to smite off the head of anyone so malign and perverse as to dispute the infallible reasoning of Doctor Truentius.

"After a couple of years of this, Truentius, finding that such domestic problems as the production and distribution of wealth and the reconciliation of order with liberty stubbornly resisted the best efforts of himself and his headsman, bethought him of spreading the blessings of popular government to the rest of Twelve Cities. Besides the benefits that such a program would confer upon the other Novarians, it would rally the Vindines, who were beginning to fall into seditious factions, behind their First Consul and furnish him with a pretext for making his rule even more absolute. He therefore sent an ultimatum to King Filoman of Kortoli, demanding that Filoman abdicate in favor of a popularly elected consul.

"Naturally perturbed, King Filoman sought advice. The advice he got from his councillors, however, was so contradictory that Filoman could make nought of it. Some were for arming every man in the kingdom and resisting to the last; but others pointed out that no such stock of arms existed.

"Some said to reactivate the old army and recall the retired officers to the colors. But it transpired that most of these officers had gone abroad to seek service as mercenaries. The former general of the Kortolian army, for instance, was now serving as a captain in the forces of the Grand Bastard of Othomae. It would take too long to recall them, even if they were willing to come.

"Old Periax urged Filoman to yield to Truentius' overwhelming force. But others said that, judging by his master's conduct, the new First Consul's first act would be to set up a chopping block in Kortoli City to shorten everybody who might possibly be a threat to him, which included all those present.

"At last it was decided to make some arms, and buy some, and call up the lustier young men, and hire such former officers as could be found to train them to use them.

"The only thing that saved Kortoli from conquest during this parlous time was the fact that Truentius, too, had his military troubles. For most of the officers of the Vindine army, as members of the old regime, either had been executed or had fled. Truentius knew that the mob of mechanics and merchants, with whose help he had seized power, would not be up to a real campaign without much organization and training.

"To gain time, Filoman was urged to seek a parley with Consul Truentius. To strengthen Filoman's hand, it was decided to hold a plebiscite of all adult male Kortolians, as to whether they wished to continue under the rule of King Filoman or to change to a republican system like that of Vindium. When the plebiscite was held, the Kortolians gave Filoman ninety-seven out of every hundred votes. This may have been the voters' honest opinion, since Filoman was then greatly beloved for his modesty, kindliness, and other virtues. Besides, Truentius' republican doctrines had been somewhat discredited by tales of his unbridled use of the ax.

"The question also arose, who should command the new Kortolian army? Several councillors put themselves forward for the post. But, whenever one proposed himself, the others shouted him down, crying that he was an ambitious schemer who sought to use his power to usurp the throne. So vehement was the opposition to any name proposed that Filoman felt he needs must leave his choice in abeyance for the time being.

"The parley with Truentius was duly arranged. It took place on an islet in the river Posaurus, which divided Vindium from Kortoli. Each was to bring no more than three armed men with him. In due course, the two met, ate lunch, and got down to business. Truentius said:

"'My good Filoman, love you your people?'

"'Certes!' replied the king. 'Have I not proven it an hundred times over?'

"'Then, an you truly love them, you must yield your throne as I have demanded. Otherwise you will bring down upon them a brutal, sanguinary war. The choice is yours, and so is the responsibility.'

"'And wherefore should I do that?'

"'First, because I demand it and have the force to compel your compliance; second, because it is the good and righteous thing to do. Monarchy is an ancient superstition, an outmoded charade, an obsolete form of injustice and oppression.' And Truentius lectured Filoman on the reasons for a popular republic.

"'But,' said Filoman, 'we have just polled the Kortolians, and they voted overwhelmingly to keep the monarchy.'

"Truentius laughed. 'My dear Filoman, do you expect me to take your vote seriously, when you held the plebiscite and counted the votes?'

"'Do you insinuate that I cheated?' cried Filoman in wrath. 'Never has anyone so impugned my honesty in the five years of my reign!'

"Truentius merely laughed some more. 'Well, let us suppose that you did report the votes truthfully. You are a naïve enough young fool to have done just that. It still makes no difference, since the *people* natheless voted for a republic.'

"'How do you make that?'

"'Why, it is simple. Any population is divided into two factions: the people, and the enemies of the people.

Since my program is the best one for the people, anybody who opposes it must logically be an enemy of the people.'

"'Mean you,' said Filoman, 'that if ninety-seven out of every hundred vote for me and three for you, the three are the people and the other ninety-seven the enemies thereof?'

"'Certes, my lad. Right glad am I to see that you learn the facts of politics so quickly.'

"'But that is absurd!' cried Filoman. 'It is merely a pretext for the infinite expansion of your own power!'

"Truentius sighed. 'I will try once more to explain, albeit I fear your grasp of logic is inadequate. My guiding principle is: all power to the people. The people, I assume, are always right. Do you follow me so far?'

"'Aye.'

"'Then, if certain malevolent or misguided persons make a decision that is obviously wrong, it follows that they cannot belong to the people. Therefore they must be enemies of the people.'

"'But who decides which decision is right?'

"'No mere mortal mind decides that, but the iron laws of logic. For ensample, I have explained to you why a republican government is preferable to a monarchy. This is an objective fact, which no personal whim, error, or bias can alter, any more than they can change the sum of two and two. Therefore—'

"But Filoman interrupted: 'Never! I will die fighting ere I suffer you to put this monstrous doctrine into effect!"

"'Oh, come, my dear King! That is quite unnecessary. You can abdicate and flee abroad with as much of the royal treasury as you can bear with you. In fact, I have your successor, the First Consul of Kortoli, already chosen. He is a muleteer named Knops: a good man who will promote your former people's welfare.'

"'The people would never vote your puppet Knops into office!'

"'Oh, yes they would, because he would have no opposition. Since I have chosen him, and since my logic is irrefutable, it follows that Master Knops is the best man for the magistracy. Anybody opposing him would be an enemy of the people, to be slain out of hand.'

" 'But Knops is not even a Kortolian!'

" 'Not now; but as your last official act, you can confer citzenship upon him. I like to keep things orderly—'

"Just then, a powerful sneeze came from a clump of alders on the Vindine side of the Posaurus. Filoman looked up, startled, and his eyes caught the glint of the sun on steel. For once he acted with admirable promptitude. He shouted to his men-at-arms: 'Treason! Let us fly!' And he and his men sprang to their feet and ran through the shallows to the Kortolian side of the river, where a groom held their horses.

"Truentius' guards and the men he had hidden rushed after them and brought down one of Filoman's men with an arrow; but the king and the others got away. It had not occurred to Filoman to have more armed men waiting over the nearest hill to come to his aid, so there was nought to do but ride hell-for-leather. They galloped off into the hills of southern Kortoli and lost their pursuers.

"They lost themselves, also. They were wandering around, suffering hunger and thirst, when a woman of early middle years called to them from a hillside.

" 'Hail, Your Majesty!' she cried. 'Can a loyal subject be of service to you?'

" 'Methinks you can, good lady,' quoth Filoman. 'But how know you me?'

" 'I have powers not of this mundane sphere,' she said. 'But come on into my cave and refresh yourselves.'

" 'Mean you that you are a witch?'

" 'Nay, sire; a proper wizardess, hight Gloé. At least, I should be but for a trifle of difficulty about my license, which I am sure Your Majesty can put straight with a snap of his finger.'

"When Filoman, his two surviving men-at-arms, and the groom had refreshed themselves, Filoman said: 'I am sure the difficulty whereof you speak can be ironed out. But if you have in sooth magical powers, mayhap you can tell me how to find a commander-in-chief for

101

my new army, which is even now drilling against the expected onslaught from Vindium.'

"Then he told her how, amongst his councillors, all those with warlike experience—and some without—coveted the post, but none wished for anyone else to have it. In sooth, King Filoman himself worried over the prospect that a successful general might oust him from his throne.

"'Why not lead your army yourself?' asked Gloé.

"'I am not qualified. Being a lover of peace and of my fellow men, I have not sought experience with the bloody art of war.'

"'Well, then,' said Gloé, 'I needs must make you a golem general.'

"'A what?'

"'A golem is a manlike image of clay, animated by a demon from the Fifth Plane. I shall set this demon the task of defeating the Vindines. I shall promise him that, once that is done, he may return to his own plane, leaving the image lifeless and no threat to Your Majesty. If you would fain preserve the image, you can bake it to brick and stand it on a pedestal.'

"'But,' said Filoman, 'will this demon of yours possess the needful military skill?'

"'He will be adequate, sire. After all, the Vindine army is itself but a rabble of shopkeepers and artisans, since most of the Vindine knightly class who have not lost their heads have fled abroad. Moreover, Truentius, for all his bloodthirsty talk, is an arrant coward who cannot bear the sight of blood. He never attends those executions he orders so lavishly.'

"This seemed like a sound proposal, so Filoman assented. A sennight later, Gloé arrived in Kortoli City driving an oxcart wherein, padded by straw against damage, lay the image of a man seven feet tall. When the cart drew up in front of the palace, Gloé uttered a spell. Then the image threw off its straw and climbed creakily to its feet.

"It was the image of a mighty warrior in armor, wearing the insignia of a Kortolian general. Gloé had not stinted her preparations, for the clay that composed the armor and costume of the image was painted to resemble the real thing. In fact, one had to look closely to perceive that it was not in sooth a normal man of commanding aspect.

"In a hoarse, growling voice, the image said: 'General Golemius reporting for duty, Your Majesty.'

"And indeed, General Golemius proved a competent commander, even if the yellow-gray complexion of his face and hands made the soldiers uneasy.

"Another sennight passed, and word came that the Vindines had crossed the Posaurus into southern Kortoli. Filoman and his new army marched out to meet them. Filoman kept in the background and left the active commanding to General Golemius, who seemed to manage well enough.

"At length the two armies sighted each other, on a dank day of lowering clouds. General Golemius drew up his army. Filoman, mounted and attended by a small personal guard, watched admiringly from a nearby hilltop.

"When the golem general had gotten all his men in place, he stepped to the fore, waved his sword, and growled: 'Forward!' So the army clattered after their general, who tramped stolidly in the lead.

"Filoman walked his horse down the hill and followed the army at a leisurely pace. The force marched across the plain, which was broken here and there by a few small clumps of trees. As the two armies approached, Filoman saw that which startled him. Leading the Vindine army was, not First Consul Doctor Truentius, but another golem general. For Truentius, being as Gloé had said a physical coward, had had recourse to his own sorcerer. This thaumaturge had summoned another demon from the Fifth Plane to animate a general of clay.

"The armies moved slowly, because both were composed largely of green troops, whose alignment was often disordered by the trees that dotted the plain. When this happened, the two clay generals had to halt their forces and straighten them out again. And then it began to rain.

"As the armies came closer, the rain came down harder. It rang on helmets with a metallic sound; it trickled down inside hauberk and greave. And, just as the armies came within bowshot, they slowed and stopped.

"King Filoman pushed his horse forward through the rear ranks to see what had halted his host. Soon he observed that General Golemius was standing still in front of his army. Moreover, the general seemed to have lost in stature and gained in girth. As Filoman watched, the general dissolved into a mound of mud, as did the other general.

"That left both armies without commanders. Over against the Kortolians stood the Vindines, whose army was much larger. Behind the Vindine army, First Consul Truentius sat in his carriage, watching, for he had never learnt to ride a horse. When his army halted, he clambered up on the roof of his carriage to see what betid. Discovering that his general, like the other, had reverted to clay, he began to shout: 'Forward, my brave men! At them! Charge!'

"At first, his army milled and shuffled uncertainly. But then some officers, by blows and exhortations, got their units moving again.

"Meanwhile the Kortolian army, seeing a force of nearly twice their own strength bearing down upon them, began to edge backwards. Here and there a man broke from the ranks and ran. Vindine arrows began to fall amongst the Kortolians.

"King Filoman had drawn up his horse beneath a tree, to keep out of the rain. And in this tree was a hornets' nest. Because of the rain, the hornets were all huddled inside their nest and minding their own affairs, when an arrow aimed at the king flew high and skewered their nest. I know not if Penembei have insects like these, but our Novarian hornets most fiercely resent any tampering with their nests and take stern measures against the tamperer.

"As the hornets swarmed out, the first animate thing they beheld was King Filoman. He was sitting his horse right under their bough, waving his sword and trying by cries and appeals to stem the rout of his army, in much the same vein as Truentius on the other side was harkening on his host. Presently Filoman gave an even louder yell as a hornet stung him on the wrist and another on the cheek. Then his horse whinnied, as another stung it on the arse, and bounded forward.

"Filoman's guard put spurs to their steeds to keep up with the king. The soldiers saw their king galloping straight at the foe, brandishing his sword and followed by a handful of bodyguards. Someone set up a cry of: 'Save the king!' and started running after Filoman. When some did, all did, so that what had been a rout of the Kortolians was changed in a trice into a rout of the Vindines.

"Truentius commanded his coachman to turn the carriage around; but, finding this difficult in the press, the coachman lighted down from his seat and fled on foot. Truentius then climbed into the driver's seat and tried to take the reins himself. Having no knowledge of chariotry, however, he was unable to bring the frightened horses under control. Then he got down, too, but was overborne in the rout and trampled to death.

"The Vindines fled in disorder from Kortoli. When the survivors got home, they changed their constitution to allow for two elected consuls, in the hope that the twain would watch each other and keep each other from seizing unlawful power. And, despite interludes of turbulence and usurpation, they have kept to that scheme ever since.

"Filoman rode home in triumph, notwithstanding that his face was grotesquely swollen from the sting. He was hailed as the savior of Kortoli for his desperate charge into the heart of the foe. He disclaimed credit, saying that the victor was neither himself nor his golem general, but the hornet that had stung his horse's rump. But so great was the love for Filoman that people said, ah, that is just our hero-king being modest.

"In any case, Filoman decided to stick to flesh-and-blood generals thereafter. They might have their faults but at least would not dissolve into mud at the first wetting.

"Later, Filoman's reign became more and more eccentric. He retained a ghost as his minister; he tried to abolish crime by pensioning all criminals; and he fell under the influence of a Mulvanian ascetic, Ajimbalin. This man persuaded him to lead a life of utter self-denial and mortification of the flesh, to the neglect of his kingdom and of his queen, who eloped with a pirate captain.

"The Kortolians sometimes wondered if they had not been wiser to toss Filoman out and adopt a republican scheme like that urged upon them by Truentius. In fact, they might well have done so; but, ere matters could come to a head, Filoman lost his life in a riding accident and was succeeded by his much abler son Fusinian. King Fusinian restored the popularity of the monarchy, and it has persisted down to the present day."

The king laughed heartily until he got into a fit of coughing and wheezing and had to be slapped on the back by his taster and his secretary.

"At least," he said, "we have never appointed a general of clockwork or of clay, heh heh. Chuivir may not be any Juktar the Great, but at least he bleeds if one pricks him." The king's little black eyes stared sharply at Jorian out of his puffy, round face. "That brings up a problem. Yes, sir, a problem. Two days ago, our spies brought us a rumor that you, dear boy, were not quite what you seemed—that, in sooth, you were no mere mechanic but a former ruler of some Novarian city-state. Is that true?"

Jorian and Karadur exchanged glances. Jorian muttered: "Zerlik must have been flapping that long tongue of his." He turned to the king. "It is true, Your Majesty. Your servant was king of Xylar for five years. Know you their method of succession?"

"We once knew but have forgotten. Tell us."

"Every five years, they come together in a grand assembly, cut off the old king's head, and throw it up for grabs. I became king by catching my predecessor's head when I saw it flying towards me, not then realizing what the object was and what catching it implied. When my five years neared their end, Doctor Karadur devised a method for me to escape this drastic ritual."

"Bountiful heavens!" exclaimed the king. "Here, the ruler is at least granted more than five years of tenure; albeit the principle is not wholly different. How did the Xylarians take the escape of their human toss-ball?"

"They have been after me ever since, to drag me back and complete their interrupted ceremony. Therefore I beg Your Majesty not to reveal my former status, lest the Xylarians get wind of my whereabouts and kidnap me. I barely escaped one such attempt on my way hither."

The king clucked. "Too bad, too bad. An we could publicly proclaim that you were a former king, we could do fine things for you. What was the date of your birth?"

Jorian raised his bushy black eyebrows, but replied: "I was born in the twelfth year of King Fealin the Second of Kortoli, on the fifteenth of the Month of the Lion. Why, sire?"

"Have you taken that down, Herekit?" the king asked his secretary; then to Jorian: "We asked it so that our wise men can calculate what the fates have in store for you. Tell me: had you warlike experience during your kingship?"

"Aye, sire; quite a lot. I led Xylar's army in two pitched battles, at Dol and at Larunum, with brigands calling themselves free companies, as well as several skirmishes. I admiraled the Xylarian fleet in driving the Algarthian pirates away from our shores. Besides, I had already seen battle whilst serving a hitch in the Foot Guards of the Grand Bastard of Othomae."

"Then, my dear Jorian, you would seem to be the answer to a fat old man's prayer."

"How so, sire?"

"Look you. We know nought of warfare and make no pretense of doing so. Our senior officer, Colonel Chuivir, is, for practical purposes, as ignorant as we. He, howsomever, is not fain to admit it. For that matter, it would do the spirits of the defenders no good for their commander to avouch himself a military ninny.

"We lack time to find a replacement for Chuivir.

Most of the officers in his command are, we suspect, as innocent of war as he. Our seasoned commanders are all with the frontier army. Nor can we appoint you in Chuivir's place. You are a foreigner and a commoner, whom the militia would not obey with any zeal. Moreover, Chuivir has influential friends among the nobility and officials, who would be affronted by our abruptly dismissing him ere he has had time to commit any gross blunder. Even a king with theoretically unlimited power, you know, must constantly make sure of his political support, heh heh."

"Well, sire?" said Jorian as Ishbahar hesitated.

"So we—ah—the thought has come to us: How would you like to be our military aide?"

"What would that entail?"

"Oh, you would wear a fancy uniform. In theory, you would be merely our messenger boy, to carry our commands to the forces and bring us reports of the fighting. In practice, we shall ask you to look over the military situation every day, decide what needs to be done, and advise us accordingly. We shall put your recommendations in the form of royal commands, which you shall convey to Chuivir or whomever else we designate. You will not seem to have any power over the defense but in fact will be in full command thereof. How does that strike you?"

"All I can say, sire, is that I will try my best."

"Good." Ishbahar spoke to the secretary: "Herekit! Draw up a commission for Master Jorian—yes, Ebeji?"

"Sire," said the attendant, who had just come in, "a ship's officer would speak with you on urgent business."

"Oh, curse this churlish world, that will not let a man eat a simple snack in peace! Send him in."

The visitor was a young naval officer with a drawn, ghastly look, who dropped to one knee. "Sire!"

"Well, sir?"

"Admiral Kyar is lost, and the pirates of Algarth are upon us!"

"Eh? Eh? Oh, good gods! How did this happen?"

"The—the admiral took the flagship *Ressam* out

this morn for exercises, accompanied by two small dispatch galleys, the *Onuech* and the *Byari*. At sea, we encountered a patch of fog, which some said had the look of sorcerous fog. Then, of a sudden, a swarm of Algarthian craft sped out of the fog and surrounded the *Ressam*. Being undermanned, she could not work up enough speed to fight clear. The freebooters also took the *Onuech*; but the *Byari*, by putting the marines on the oars, won free."

"Were you in command of the *Byari*?" asked the king.

"Aye, sire. If Your Majesty thinks I ought to have stayed and perished with the admiral—"

"Nay, nay, you did right. Someone had to bring us word. In fact, you are hereby promoted to admiral in place of Kyar. Prepare the rest of our navy for battle." To the secretary, the king said: "Draw up a royal commission for this officer and bring it to us to sign. Now, Admiral, do sit down and try some of this—by Ughroluk's toenails, the young man has fainted! Pour water on him, somebody!"

That evening, Jorian and Karadur stood on the floor of the Tower of Kumashar that housed the clockwork. They looked towards the sea, where the Penembic navy was locked in battle with a fleet of Algarthian pirates. The largest Penembic ships, the huge catamarans, were not even sent into action for want of rowers to man them. The ships that did take part in the battle moved sluggishly for lack of oar power.

"There goes another one," said Jorian as ruddy flames enveloped a ship.

"One of ours or theirs?" said Karadur.

"One of ours, I fear; but 'tis hard to be sure in this failing light."

"How did that young fellow—what's his name—the officer whom the king of a sudden promoted to admiral, how effective has he proven?"

Jorian shrugged. "Considering the generally unprepared state of the fleet and the lack of time, there's no way to tell. Not even Diodis of Zolon, the greatest Novarian sea commander, could have done much in this man's room."

"How do you with Colonel Chuivir?"

"Methinks he suspects the true state of affairs. He seems to take the king's commands with ill grace, even if he had not yet flouted any of them. What worries me is that, if he learn that the Xylarians are after me, he may get word to them to come and take me."

"They could hardly do that, with the city surrounded and under siege."

"True, Doctor. So I'm in a pretty pass, am I not? I'm safe whilst the siege lasts. My duty, howsomever, is to defeat and break it, which will place me again in jeopardy. If on the other hand the besiegers take the city, I shall probably lose my head in that case, too." He reached up and tugged at his head. "Just making sure 'tis firmly fixed in place."

"An we win here, I am sure the king could protect you."

"Perhaps, perhaps. But suppose he find himself straightened for money to pay the cost of the war and hear of the price the Xylarians have placed on my head?"

"Oh, he is a kindly man—"

"For the present; but the day may come when he loves his little Jorian less than the cash I could bring. My taste of kingship has taught me never to trust any ruler. They can always justify any perfidy by saying, 'It's for the people's good.'"

The battle continued for hours in ever-deepening darkness and confusion. Then the surviving Penembic ships broke off and fled up the Lyap. The pirates swept the decks of the anchored ships, both naval and merchant, and invested the shoreline outside the wall of the city.

Next day, a Free Company in flashing armor marched down the Novarian Road from the north; Mazsan's peasant army straggled up from the south; and a swarm of robed, camel-riding nomads from Fedirun approached from the east. The siege had begun.

110

✠✠✠✠✠✠✠✠✠✠✠✠✠✠

VII

THE SIEGE OF IRAZ

THE BESIEGERS SPREAD AROUND IRAZ, OUT OF CATAPULT range, and set up their camps. That of the Free Company was an orderly fortified square of tents, surrounded by a ditch and an embankment. It stood in the fields northeast of the city, where a bend in the Lyap gave the mercenaries room to camp between the river and the wall.

The camp of the Fedirunis was a sprawling city of brown camel's hair tents set every which way, whence sounds of drums and wailing music arose at night. From eastward, a stream of Fedirunis rode camels, horses, mules, and asses down the East Road to join the besiegers. The news that Iraz might be sacked had spread over the eastern deserts and had drawn all the sand thieves of Fedirun like flies to honey. The city of camel's-hair tents grew and spread like a fungus.

Mazasan's peasants had not brought tents. Instead, they built rude huts of fieldstone and brushwood or else slept, bundled in sheepskins, in the open. The Algarthian pirates slept aboard their ships.

The suburb of Zaktan across the Lyap, whose people had all fled to Iraz proper, was plundered and some of the houses were burnt; but a rainy spell prevented a general conflagration. The beacon atop the Tower of Kumashar was dark, for the only incoming ships were additions to the pirate fleet.

The besiegers assembled mantlets, which they extended in lines towards the city. From behind these defenses, their archers sniped at Irazis on the walls.

111

Since this part of Penembei had few trees, the besiegers' engineers broke up some of King Ishbahar's biggest war galleys for timber to build their engines.

Beyond the lines of mantlets, siege engines—catapults, tortoises (wheeled sheds), and belfries (movable siege towers)—began to take shape. The sounds of sawing and hammering continued day and night.

Meanwhile, the wizards on both sides tried out their arts. The besiegers' magicians conjured up illusions of vast, winged monsters, which swooped with bared fangs and fiery breath at the battlements. At first, the defenders scattered with cries of alarm. But Karadur and his assistant wizards quickly identified these monsters as mere harmless phantasms and dispersed them with counter-spells.

The besiegers' sorcerers then cast a mighty spell, which evoked a horde of bat-winged, scaly demons from the Sixth Plane, to assail the defenders with fangs and talons. But the defending thaumaturgists cast a counter-spell. This spell caused all the bees, wasps, and hornets within ten leagues of Iraz to swarm to the city and attack the demons. With shrieks of pain and croaks of outrage, the demons fled and vanished back to their own plane.

The men of the Free Company, as the best-disciplined soldiers among the attackers, were the first to complete a catapult. The skeins, slings, and fittings they had brought along in their baggage wagons, and for timbers they used wood from the dismantled battleships.

This catapult was of the two-armed, dart-throwing type. They levered it forward on its ponderous wheels. A big wooden shield, hung with green hides, was fastened in front of it to protect it against counter-bombardment. Karadur's wizards, collected on the wall, sweated and mumbled and gesticulated in attempts to cast a spell upon the device.

Early one morning, under an overcast sky, Karadur stood watching from the wall. He said to Jorian: "I fear me, alas, that they have already placed a protective spell over yonder engine, so that all my wizards' efforts will go for nought. The advances in magic of recent centuries have given the defense great advantages in wizardly conflict."

Jorian, in silvered scale mail, peered through his spyglass. "Methinks they're ready to shoot," he said. "Take a look."

"Ah, me! You are right."

"Get ready to duck. One of those darts would skewer you like an olive on a toothpick... Here it comes!"

The Free Company's catapult discharged with a crash. The missile—a three-foot bolt of wood and iron, with wooden vanes—whistled over their heads, to curve down and fall inside the city.

"If that be the best they can do," said Karadur, "I doubt that they will soon beat us down by hurling darts at random into this vast city."

"You don't understand," said Jorian. "That was a mere ranging shot. When they get the elevation right, they'll use that engine to scatter defenders on the wall and thus hinder the servicing of our engines. Now, do you see that other catapult a-building, back of the first one?"

"Aye."

"That one will be twice as big and will throw balls of stone or brick instead of darts. They'll wheel it forward and set it to battering a breach in our wall, whilst the dart-thrower protects it 'gainst our counter-measures by a covering bombardment. It may take a fortnight; but soon or late, the wall will crumble and fall at that point."

"What can we do?"

"I've already told Colonel Chuivir to start his masons building a lune behind the threatened point. Whether he'll do it is another thing. He suspects that, when I tell him 'tis the king's will that he do thus-and-so, it is really my idea, and he bubbles with resentment."

"How is our defending army coming?"

Jorian spat. "Lousy! The Royal Guard have had at least formal training, but they're a mere handful. The militia companies are drilling; but the two stasiarchs are more interested in blackguarding and plotting against each other than they are in winning the war. There have been many affrays betwixt Pants and Kilts, with several wounded and a couple slain.

"They're just urban rabble anyway: splendid at rioting, looting, and arson, but as soldiers worth no more than so many rabbits. They argue every command and take a perverse pride in slovenliness and indiscipline. Had I but a few thousand of my sturdy Kortolian peasants..." Jorian laughed shortly. "Perdy, kimmer," he said, falling into his rustic Kortolian dialect, "a grew up in little Ardamai and kenned the farm folk well. Then a thought them the crassest clods, dullards, and skinflints on earth. When a first saw Kortoli City, a said, aha! City life be the life for me! And indeed, a still find city folk better company. But, when it come to the push of the pike, gie me yeomen wi' dung on their boots and na thought but the next harvest in their heads!

"Now, take those houses built against the West Wall, along the waterfront street. That was strictly illegal, since such dwellings provide cover for attackers; but Ishbahar's inspectors doubtless pocketed bribes to overlook..."

Jorian fell silent for a moment while he swept the besiegers' lines with his telescope. Then he said: "Were I boss of yon besiegers, 'stead of wasting time in building catapults and belfries, I'd make hundreds of scaling ladders and send the whole force against our walls at once."

"Why, my son? Such ladders are easily overthrown, to the scathe of the men clinging to them. I have never understood how any number of men could take a defended wall. Why cannot the defenders simply push over the ladders as fast as they are erected?"

"Were numbers anywhere near even, they could. Stout-hearted defenders can beat off several times their number of attackers. But the foe now outnumber us fifteen or twenty to one—at least as far as real soldiers are concerned; I count not Vegh's and Amazluek's rabble. With the defenders so few, they could not man all parts of the wall at once. By throwing up ladders against parts of the wall that are bare for the nonce, the assailants can get a lodgment on the top. Once a few sections are taken, the attackers can stream down into the city and make their numbers felt.

"If the foe strike now, he'll have an excellent chance of overrunning the city; whereas, an he fool around with all these beautiful engines, he may find his advantage lost by Tereyai's arrival...Speaking of whom, has your scryer, what's his name, found out whether our messengers have yet reached General Tereyai?"

"Nedef has been at his crystal from dawn to sunset, but the scrying has been poor. I daresay the foe's wizards have cast spells to block it. Now and then Nedef gets a fix on some spot in northern Penembei, but all he sees are bare brown hills, with no sign either of our frontier army or of the messengers."

"Hmm." Jorian stared so long through his spyglass that Karadur said:

"What is it, O Jorian?"

"See you that thing between the camps of the Free Company and that of the Fedirunis?"

"It looks like another line of mantlets, does it not? My dim old eyes—"

"Aye, but what are mantlets doing so far back? Even a catapult couldn't reach 'em. They seem inordinately high, and methinks I detect activity behind them." Jorian turned on Karadur. "Could your scryer get a glimpse behind that fence?"

"He can try, whilst I essay to counter the interference of the foe's magicians."

An hour later, Jorian and Karadur sat in Nedef's chamber in the House of Learning. The scryer sat cross-legged on a bench, hunched over his crystal sphere, which rested upon a small stand of ebony carved into coiling dragons. Karadur sat, also cross-legged, on a cushion on the floor, leaning back with his eyes closed and moving his lips. Jorian sat in a chair, holding a stylus and a waxed wooden tablet. He leaned forward tensely, holding the stylus poised.

The scryer spoke just above a whisper: "The scene ripples and shifts, although it is not so confused as yesterday's...Methinks their wizards who cast interference upon me have been recalled to other tasks...Ah, now I see Iraz...The scene pitches and tosses, as if I were an insect riding an autumnal leaf borne along on the wind...Steady, steady...Nay, that is the wrong side of the besiegers' ring...Now I have the nomads' tents in view...More to the left! The left! Ah, here we are. Here is your fence, whereon I look down...Curse this interference; it is like trying to see the bottom of a river through the waters of a rapid. I see a great pile of long things; long things with crosspieces...Ah...Now I see men working on these objects...From my height, they look like ants; but...They hammer and saw..."

"Ladders?" said Jorian.

"Ah, that is it! Ladders! I could not be sure, because of bad scrying, but ladders they are."

"Can you estimate their number?" said Jorian.

"Nay; but there must be hundreds..."

Jorian looked at Karadur. "They're doing just what I said I should do in their place. The siege engines are a diversion, to make us think we have plenty of time to ready our defenses. Instead, they'll rush us early some morn with all those ladders and scramble over our walls ere we've rubbed the sleep out of our eyes. Once inside, they could stand off Tereyai for ay. With command of the sea, they could not be starved out.

"Keep Nedef at his crystal and command him to try to learn the foe's precise plans. If he could eavesdrop on a conference amongst the leaders, that might be helpful. Meanwhile, I must forth to tell Chuivir to build crutches."

"Crutches?"

"That's what we call those poles with a curved or forked crosspiece at the end, for pushing over ladders."

"Beware of arousing Chuivir's jealousy!"

Jorian had thitherto been careful to report back to the palace before issuing royal commands to Colonel Chuivir. But, as he strode through the streets between the House of Learning and the palace, an uproar drew his attention. A group of armed Kilts was chasing three Pants along the avenue, waving swords and shouting vengeance.

"Heryx blast them!" snarled Jorian to himself, stepping out into the street. As the Pants ran past him, he threw out his arms in a commanding gesture and roared: "Halt, in the king's name!"

At least, he thought, his glittering parade armor did have its uses. At the sight of his regalia, the pursuing Kilts halted. The three Pants clustered behind him, panting:

"They...would...slay us...good sir! And...for nought!"

"What is all this?" barked Jorian.

"Thieves!" screamed the leading Kilt. "We found them sneaking and snooping around our armory, to steal our weapons!"

"They lie!" cried a new voice. Jorian turned, and there was the plump Lord Vegh, stasiarch of the Pants. "I sent my trusty lads thither to ask a few civil questions of the other faction, as to what armament they thought most suitable—"

"Now it is ye who lie!" cried the gaunt, goateed Amazluek, pushing through the gathering crowd. "Civil questions, forsooth! Mere questioners need not try to pick the lock on the armory door—"

"There was no one on guard," shouted a Pant. "None to answer our questions, so we sought to—"

Amazluek: "Liar again! There is always a man—"

"Thou callest me liar?" yelled Vegh, drawing his sword.

"Liar, thief, and coward!" screamed Amazluek, drawing likewise.

"Stop it! Stop it!" shouted Jorian over the rising din. "Put up your blades, in the king's name!"

The clash and ring of sword against sword answered him. Spectators began to shout and to cheer on the combatants according to which faction they supported. They also began to bark threats and insults at each

117

other. Jorian saw one man kick another's shins, another tweak another's nose, and a third seize another's hair and pull it. A full street battle was in the making. In desperation, Jorian drew his sword and knocked up the crossed blades of the stasiarchs.

"Keep out of this, dirty foreigner!" snarled Amazluek, making a thrust at Jorian's chest. Not expecting the attack, Jorian was slow in parrying. But his corselet saved his life as the stasiarch's point skittered off its scales and tore the sleeve of Jorian's jacket.

Vegh lunged at Amazluek, who had to leap back and make a hasty parry to save his own gore. Jorian unhooked his lead-pommeled dagger. Holding it by the sheath, he stopped behind Amazluek and brought the pommel down on the stasiarch's head.

Amazluek wilted to the cobblestones. When Vegh made to run the prostrate man through, Jorian knocked his blade aside and thrust his own point into Vegh's face.

"Get back, or I will give you some of the same!" he said.

"Who are you to order us about—" sputtered Vegh.

"I am who I am. You five Kilts, carry Lord Amazluek back to your headquarters. If water in the face fail to revive him, fetch a chirurgeon to tend him. Lord Vegh, will you be so good as to send your men back to their barracks? Meseems they need every waking hour for drill, if they are to withstand the foe."

The Kilts, cowed by Jorian's size and air of command, silently picked up their fallen leader and disappeared. Vegh grumbled some threat or curse under his breath. Being a full head shorter than Jorian, he seemed indisposed to carry the argument further. He and his trio also departed, and the crowd broke up.

Jorian hurried on to the palace. The sun had passed the meridian, and Jorian felt oppressed by the need for haste. The attack with scaling ladders might come at any time, and the disparity in numbers of hardened fighters grew with every additional Fediruni who halted his camel in the growing tent city east of Iraz.

It was urgent that the crutches be prepared forthwith. It was also urgent that something drastic be done about the command of the militia, before the factions began a civil war.

At the palace, Jorian was told that King Ishbahar was taking his nap after lunch and could not be disturbed. Jorian chewed his mustache in frustration. He considered forcing an entrance to the king's private chambers on grounds of emergency, waiting until the king awoke, or going directly to Chuivir without clearing his intentions with the king first. The dangers of the last course seemed to him the least.

He found the handsome colonel in his chamber in the topmost level of the huge, cylindrical keep built against the wall on the eastern side of the city. Thence Chuivir could watch the entire length of the East Wall, including the East Gate. Chuivir, wearing gilded lizard mail even more gorgeous than Jorian's, was checking payrolls.

Jorian saluted by bringing his fist to his chest. "Colonel," he said, "it is the king's pleasure that his forces prepare for an imminent assault on the walls by scaling ladders. In particular, he desires that hundreds of crutches be prepared and placed on the walls to overthrow these ladders."

Chuivir frowned. "Where got he any such idea, Captain Jorian? Any fool can see that they are readying a prolonged attack on the walls themselves, by catapults and ram tortoises, in order to make a breach before mounting his assault."

Jorian told of the scryer's discovery of the ladder work going on behind the fence to the northeast. Colonel Chuivir picked up his own spyglass and leaned out the window on that side of the tower. After a while, he said:

"Nay, your seer must have been mistaken. Even if they be preparing ladders, it were incredible that they should essay to use them so early upon our walls."

"His Majesty," said Jorian, "thinks they are fain to make a sudden assault in hope of carrying the city ere General Tereyai arrive with his army."

Chuivir stubbornly stuck to his point. "My good Captain, it says right here in Zayuit's *Military Manual*"—he waved a copy—"that the chances of carrying a wall over forty feet high with ladders alone were negligible. And our walls measure forty-five feet."

"A city this size should have at least sixty-foot walls," said Jorian.

"Perhaps; but that is beside the point."

"Well, are you going to set men to making crutches?"

"No. I need all the manpower I can get for practise at conventional drill, for arms making, and for strengthening the masonry."

"But, sir, His Majesty was quite positive—"

The colonel gave Jorian a sharp look. "Meseems that, to listen to you, His Majesty has been taking an entirely unwonted interest in the details of the defense—something he has never done hitherto. Did he give you such a message just now, from his own mouth?"

"Certes. You do not think I would give you orders on my own responsibility, do you?"

"On the contrary, that is just what I think. Know, good my sir, that I command the defense and none other—let alone foreign interlopers. If you would convince me that His Majesty has in sooth issued this silly command, you must bring me a written order in his own hand, or else persuade him to issue his dicta to me in person."

"Would you rather let the enemy in than yield on a bit of protocol?" said Jorian angrily. "If I must needs run back and forth all day bearing bits of paper—."

"Get out of here!" shouted Chuivir. "Any royal commands hereafter shall be in writing, or I will ignore them. Now off with you and stop pestering me, or I will have you arrested!"

"We shall see," growled Jorian. He left the tower fuming.

That evening over supper, he told Karadur of the day's events.

"When I got back to the palace," he said, "I found the King just waking up. I told him about the quarreling between the factions and about my troubles with Chui-vir. I said I feared my supervision would come to nought unless I had direct and acknowledged command of the whole defense, with none to gainsay me. Even then, 'twould be a chancy thing.

"I told Ishbahar I wanted nothing less than commanding the defense of Iraz, which was not my city; but I was caught therein and stood to fall therewith. Hence, to save my own hide, I needs must do what I could to save it."

"Did he believe your—ah—protestations of virtue?"

"I know not, albeit they expressed my true sentiments. He flat refused, howsomever, to oust Chuivir and the stasiarchs and appoint me in their room, saying 'twere politically impossible.

"At length he summoned the three and me to tea this afternoon. Another gorge, naturally. If His Majesty keep on stuffing me like a sausage skin, I shall have to go on a fast; I've already gained ten pounds in Iraz.

"Well, at table, Amazluek, with a bandage round his head, glared daggers at Vegh and me. But I will say old Fatty did his best. He homilized us on the need for coöperation whilst the siege lasted. An we failed to work together, he reminded us, we should be tied to posts, tarred, and kindled to illumine the Fedirunis' victory feast. The desert dwellers have quaint notions of entreating their captives. At the end, he was blub-bering great tears of self-pity and had even my three recalcitrant commanders looking solemn and wiping their eyes."

"Did he confirm your tale of having obtained the order about the crutches from him?"

"Aye; luckily, I had thought to prime him on this little white lie. So we all parted with expressions, if not of good will, at least of promises to work for the common goal. But nought has really been changed, and the morrow will doubtless see us at one another's throats again."

"How about those crutches?"

"Seeing a chance to score off his rival, Amazluek

121

said he'd be responsible for them. His faction, he said, had many competent woodworkers, and he would set them to sawing and nailing night and day. Then Vegh said his Pants could make two crutches for every one turned out by the Kilts. The king said to go to it."

Karadur: "My son, I promised Nedef to look in at his sanctum this even. He is attempting to spy on a meeting of the hostile commanders, to learn what he can of their plans. Wilt—ah—accompany me? With all in confusion and arms handed out broadcast, the streets are none too safe o' nights."

"Surely, old man. Have you a lanthorn?"

Nedef murmured: "Nay, I see no gathering around the tent of the Fediruni chieftain ... That leaves the Algarthians ..."

For some minutes, the scryer sat silently with an intense expression, as he strove to guide the vision in the crystal seaward.

"It is easier this even," he said. "Belike all the wizards are at meat. Ah, here is the pirates' flagship, with longboats clustering about her. The council of war must be aboard ..." Then more silence. Nedef gasped: "Aid me, Doctor Karadur! The wizards have cast a protective spell about the admiral's cabin, so I cannot enter it."

Karadur mumbled and made passes. At last Nedef exclaimed: "Ah, now I am in! But it takes all my strength to remain ..."

"What see you?" asked Jorian.

"In sooth, it is a veritable council of war. I see Mazsan the factionist, and the pirate admiral—I think his name is Hrundikar, a great huge wight with a long red beard. I also see the leaders of the Free Company and of the nomads, whose names I know not."

"What do they?"

"They talk, with much gesticulation and pauses for the interpreters ... Mazsan says something about making an attack from all four sides at once, to stretch the defense thin ..."

Silence, then: "They argue the question of timing their attack. The Fediruni points heavenward; he—I

122

cannot read his lips, for he speaks his native tongue. Ah, the interpreter asks how they can time their attacks with the sun hidden by clouds...

"Now Mazsan speaks. He says something about the Tower of Kumashar...He holds a spyglass to his eye. The Fediruni asks a question, but I cannot catch it...Mazsan demands something of Admiral Hrundikar. Everybody takes a drink...Now a sailor brings in a sheet of something—parchment or paper. They spike it to the bulkhead; each of the four chieftains drives his dagger through one corner of the sheet. With a piece of charcoal, Mazsan draws a two-foot circle on the sheet. He marks a spot in the enter. He makes a set of marks around the edge of the circle. He draws an arrow, starting at the center and pointing to one of the marks..."

"Which mark? Which mark?" demanded Jorian.

"It is on the right-hand side of the circle...My vision is blurred..."

"If it were a clock, what time would it tell?"

"Ah, I see! The clock hand points to the third hour. Now the scene grows wavery, as if their wizards had returned to their task..."

Nedef's voice trailed off. The scryer slumped in a faint and rolled off his bench to the floor.

"Dear me, I hope he have not damaged his brain," said Karadur. "That is a hazard of his profession."

"His pulse seems normal," said Jorian, bending over the fallen man. "So now we know: the foe will attack at the third hour of the morning—or the Hour of the Otter, as we say in Novaria. They will time their assault by watching the Tower of Kumashar through telescopes."

"We know not the day of the attack," said Karadur.

"True, but we had better assume it to be tomorrow. I must get word to the king and the commanders."

"I cannot leave poor Nedef in a swoon..."

"Take care of him, then, whilst I go about my business, which brooks no delay."

"Go you first to the king?"

"Nay, I think I'll drop in first on Chuivir to pass the news."

"What chance have we, with a few hundred guardsmen against their tens of thousands?"

"The chance of a pollywog in a pond full of pike. But the militia can push over ladders if nought else. Still, 'tis a muchel of city wall to cover with a small force. All they need is one good foothold..."

"I suppose we could stop the clocks in the Tower of Kumashar. Then they would lack means of coördinating their attack."

Jorian stared. "You're right, old man. But, by Heryx's iron yard, you've given me an even better idea! Each of the four parties plans to attack a different side and use a different one of the four clocks, does it not?"

"I suppose so."

"All right, you succor Master Nedef; I'm off."

When he had reported to the king, who was eating a late evening snack, Ishbahar asked the same question that Karadur had already posed: "What chance have we, lad, with their twenty or thirty thousand against our four hundred-odd guardsmen and a few thousand militiamen?"

"Not much, Your Majesty," said Jorian. "I do, howsomever, have an idea that may well throw their attack into confusion."

"What is it?"

"Ere I tell Your Majesty, your servant would like to beg a boon, in case my scheme work."

"Anything, my boy, anything! If it work not, none of us will have further use for material possessions anyway. An we defeat this siege, we have plans for you."

"All I ask, sire, is your copper bathtub."

"The gods bless our soul, what an extraordinary request! No cartload of gold? No high office? No noble maiden for your harem?"

"Nay, sire; I meant just what I said."

"Of course you shall have it, win or lose. But what is your scheme?"

Jorian told him.

VIII

THE
BARBARIAN SAVIOR

As THE OVERCAST SKY PALED TO PEARLY GRAY, JORIAN told Colonel Chuivir: "The Fedirunis will attack the East Wall first, in about half an hour."

"How in the name of Ughroluk do you know?"

"Because at that time, the east clock will show the third hour."

"But will not the other clocks show the same—oh!" Chuivir stared round-eyed at Jorian. "You mean you have set them all to show different times!"

Jorian nodded, and Chuivir gave a command. Messengers departed on a run. Soon, nearly all the Royal Guard was assembled along the East Wall, with their armor gleaming dully in the gray light. Mingled with them were several companies of militia. Most of the militiamen bore either crutches or spears to whose butt-ends short crosspieces had been affixed. When all were in place, there was a man for every six feet of wall. A skeleton guard of militia was left on the other walls.

From the swarming, dun-colored camp of the Fedirunis, ram's horns gave their soft bleat. A flood of figures, robed in brown, sand color, and dirty white, poured out from the tent city and streamed towards the East Wall. They covered the earth like a swarm of ants. Foremost among them came hundreds of pairs of men, each pair carrying a ladder. Others gathered in knots and unlimbered the powerful, double-curved compound horn bows of Fedirun.

"Keep your heads down!" shouted Chuivir. The command was passed down the line.

The Fediruni bows twanged, and sheets of arrows shrieked up from their line. Some shafts soared over the battlements; others struck the stones and rebounded. A few struck home. Cries arose along the line of the defenders, and the physicians of Iraz ran up and down with their gowns flapping, seeking the wounded.

The swarm of foes flowed up to the wall. All along the line, hundreds of ladders were planted in the ground. Their other ends rose like the booms of cranes as the attackers pushed on them from behind with hands and spear points.

"Loose!" cried Chuivir.

All along the wall, arbalesters of the Royal Guard stepped out from behind their merlons to discharge their crossbows into the crowd below. Then they ducked back again to reload. Elsewhere, squads of militiamen placed boxes of heavy stones and cauldrons of boiling oil, molten lead, and red-hot sand in the embrasures and tipped them until the contents poured down on the heads beneath. Screams resounded.

Still the ladders rose until their upper ends, even with the top of the wall, came to rest.

"Wait until they are loaded, Colonel," said Jorian.

"Curse it, stop telling me how to run my business!" snapped Chuivir. "I was going to do just that." He raised his voice: "Crutch men, wait for the signal! How far up are they, Captain Jorian?"

Jorian risked a peek out an embrasure. "Three manheights. Give them a little more... Now!"

As the heads of the most active climbers approached the top of the wall, the Fediruni archers ceased shooting for fear of hitting their own. Chuivir shouted: "O-o-over!"

All along the wall, militiamen hooked their crutches into the tops of the ladders and pushed. Here and there a man fell to a Fediruni arrow, but another took his place. The ladders swayed outward and fell, dropping their shrieking burdens into the crowd.

The Fediruni leaders dashed up and down, screaming commands and exhortations. Up went the ladders again.

Again, swarms of brown-robed figures scrambled up them.

Jorian found himself next to an embrasure in front of which an Irazi militiaman had fallen with an arrow through his throat. The top of a ladder showed in the gap between the merlons. Before Jorian could gather his wits, a black-bearded brown face, surmounted by a white head cloth held in place by a camel's-hair rope, popped into the embrasure. Golden hoops hung gleaming and swaying from the man's ear lobes.

Jorian snatched up the crutch that the fallen Irazi had dropped. His first attempt to place it against one of the uprights of the ladder miscarried; he missed and almost hurled himself through the embrasure. Before he could recover and replace the implement, the Fediruni leaped like a cat through the embrasure and had at him with a scimitar.

Jorian threw up the crutch to parry a whistling cut, which drove into the wood and nearly severed the crutch. He struck at the man, but the crutch broke at its weakened point. The man slashed again; his blade clashed against Jorian's mail as Jorian leaped back.

By the time the man drew back his arm for a third blow, Jorian had his sword out. A straight thrust took the unarmored man in the ribs. The Fediruni still had the strength to complete his cut, which clanged on Jorian's helmet, knocking it down over his eyes and filling his head with stars.

Jorian pushed his helmet back into place, to see the Fediruni leaning against the merlon. The scimitar dropped from his lax fingers as the man slowly sagged to the pavement.

Meanwhile, another Fediruni had hoisted himself through the embrasure. This man carried both a scimitar and a leathern buckler in his right hand. Over his brown robe he wore a crude cuirass of boiled leather, painted red and blue, and on his head a light steel cap with a slender spike on top. As he came, he shifted the buckler to his left hand and engaged Jorian. There was a quick exchange of cuts and thrusts; the man was a skilled fighter.

Out of the corner of his eye, Jorian saw a third Fediruni, with his shaven skull bare, climbing through. If the third man gained the wall and assailed him from behind, Jorian knew he would have little chance. Despite the hero tales, it was rare indeed that a single swordsman could defeat two competent foes at once. If Jorian took his attention for a heartbeat off the man he was fighting, the fellow would instantly have him.

He tried to speed up his cuts and lunges to kill the man before the other came. But the man caught the blows on his buckler and sent back one whistling counter-cut after another...

The third man had reached the wall and slithered around behind Jorian, who knew what was happening but could do nothing to stop it. Then a shriek arose behind him, and the sound of a falling body. The eyes of the man he was fighting shifted past him, and in an instant Jorian ran him through the throat.

"Here is another!" cried Chuivir, drawing a bloody sword from the Fediruni behind Jorian. "Help me!"

The colonel referred to a fourth Fediruni, now poised on the topmost rung of the leadder with a scimitar in his teeth. Jorian and Chuivir each drove the point of his sword into one of the two uprights.

"Over!" said Chuivir.

They shoved. The ladder swayed out. It seemed to stand balanced for an incredible time, while the topmost Fediruni looked down with eyes that widened with terror in his swarthy face. The last sight that Jorian had of him, as the ladder toppled, was of the man's opening his mouth to scream and dropping the sword he had held in his teeth.

"That was close," said Chuivir. "They have gained another foothold yonder; come along!"

The two rushed along the wall to where several Fedirunis had formed a solid knot with their backs to an embrasure, while others, climbing up the ladder from behind, tried to push in.

"Watch!" said Jorian.

He put a foot on the adjacent embrasure and hurled himself up on top of the merlon. A small, slender Fediruni was just pushing through the embrasure behind the knot of battlers. At the moment, he was on hands and knees in the embrasure.

Jorian swung up his arm and brought his sword down in a long, full-armed cut. He had the satisfaction of seeing the man's head fly off, to roll among the trampling feet of the fighters. The blood-spouting body collapsed in the embrasure, and through Jorian's mind flitted a fleeting thought of wonder that so small a man should contain so much blood. A scarlet pool spread out on the flagstones, so that the fighters slipped and staggered in it.

The body hindered the next climber, who pushed and tugged at it to clear it out of the way. While he was so engaged, Jorian caught him in the face with a backhand cut. The man fell off the ladder, carrying away those below him in a whole concatenation of screams and crashes.

"Hand me a crutch!" Jorian shouted.

A spear was at length passed up to him. With this he pried one of the uprights of the ladder away from the stone and sent it toppling. The Fedirunis on the wall, cut off from support and slipping and falling in the puddles of blood, were soon beaten down and hacked to pieces.

Panting, Jorian, in dented helm and rent hauberk, confronted Colonel Chuivir, around whose left arm a physician was tying a bandage. Below, the Fedirunis sullenly flowed back towards their tent city. They carried many of their wounded; but many more were left behind, along with hundreds of corpses.

"Bad?" said Jorian.

"Scratch. You?"

"Never touched me. Thank you for your help."

"No trouble. When and whence is the next attack?" asked Chuivir.

"Soon, north. The north clock is set an hour after the east."

"The Free Company, eh?"

"Aye. Not many, but fell fighters."

"With that armor, they will not be able to climb so monkeylike. Adjutant, everybody but the skeleton guard to the North Wall!"

An hour later, the Free Company withdrew from the North Wall, leaving scores of armored figures lying like smashed beetles at its base. Jorian, bleeding from a cut on the side of his jaw, told Chuivir: "The pirates next."

The houses that had been illegally built against the West Wall, facing the waterfront, furnished the pirates with an easy means of getting halfway up the wall. They made several lodgments on the top of the wall and clung to them despite the hardest fighting; Jorian took another light wound, on his right arm. But the houses, being inflammable, soon blazed up under a shower of incendiary missiles from the wall. Pirates struggling to emplace short ladders on the roofs of the houses were engulfed in flames and died screaming.

By the time the clock on the south side of the Tower of Kumashar showed the third hour, Mazsan's peasant army had heard about the defeats of the other three forces. There was talk of a mysterious mixup in timing, and of the unexpected strength of the defenders. The yells of Mazsan's officers and even blows with the flats of swords failed to get the peasants to rush the wall. They stood sullenly muttering; some began to trickle away.

Trumpets blared in the hills. Little black specks grew to squadrons of the regular Penembic cavalry, riding down the East Road and deploying.

"Tereyai!" shouted voices along the wall, as the frontier army rolled into view.

As the word went round, Mazsan's peasants dissolved in mad flight. The Fedirunis, fearful of being cut off from their homeland, abandoned their camp, swarmed on their camels and horses, and scattered. The Algarthian pirates scrambled aboard their ships, cast off, and hoisted sail.

The Free Company struck its camp in orderly fashion. It formed three hollow squares, with pikes leveled outwards in all directions and crossbowmen inside the squares. The mercenaries marched leisurely away on the North Road, as if daring anybody to try to stop them. No one did.

"My boy!" cried the king. "You have saved Iraz! Nothing were too good for you! Nothing!"

"Oh, come, sire," said the bandaged Jorian, affecting more modesty than he really felt. "All your servant did was to sit up half the night tinkering with the clocks, to make the four dials register different hours."

"But that proves the prophecy. Or rather, both prophecies. You are the barbarian savior, and the salvation of the city depended upon the clocks' functioning—albeit not quite in the sense that one would expect, heh heh. Name your reward!"

"All I want, Your Majesty, is that copper bathtub."

"Forsooth? Well, it is a queer sort of reward; but if that is your desire, you shall have it. Shall we have it delivered to Doctor Karadur's quarters?"

"Nay, sire. Leave it where it is for the time being. But one of these days I shall want it. And one other thing!"

"Yes? Yes?"

"Pray stop calling me a barbarian! I am only an honest craftsman, as civilized as the next wight."

"Oh," said the king. "We see the difficulty. You think of a 'barbarian' as a rude, uncouth, illiterate oaf from some backward land where they know not letters and cities. But in the prophecy, methinks, the word was used in its older sense, to mean any non-Penembian. The change in meaning took place during the century preceding this one; we told you we used to be a bit of a scholar.

"So, you see, in that sense you *are* a barbarian, however refined your manners and vast your erudition. And the prophecies are proven after all. By the way, it is fortunate that our victory took place when it did, and that you sustained no grievous wounds. In three nights, we shall have a full moon again."

Jorian wrinkled his forehead. "So, Your Majesty?"

131

"Have you forgotten? That is the monthly Divine Marriage of Nubalyaga!"

"Oh," said Jorian.

Three nights later, at the full of the moon, Jorian gave the ritual knock on the massive door at the north end of Hoshcha's tunnel. The door swung open, and in it stood two minor priestesses in gauzy gowns. They bowed low, saying:

"All hail, Your Majesty, soon to be divine!"

Jorian nodded affably. "Whither away, lassies?"

"Follow us."

Jorian followed them through winding corridors, up stairs, and through portals. Once he passed the main chamber of the temple. Through an open door, he glimpsed scaffolding and saw men moving about. He heard the sounds of sawing and hammering and the clink of masons' chisels.

The Free Company and the Algarthians had looted the temple of all the gold and precious stones they could pry off the decorations. They might have destroyed the whole structure had not Mazsan's influence restrained them. Now craftsmen were working overtime to refurbish the fane.

"Priestesses!" said Jorian, "Where—ah—I mean when do I—ah—"

"Oh, sire!" murmured one. "You needs must be suitably clad ere the god incarnate himself in you!"

They led him at last into a smaller chamber, where garments were laid out on a divan.

"Now, sire," they said, "if Your Majesty will graciously sit..."

Jorian sat on the end of the divan while they pulled off his shoes and buskins.

"Now arise, sire, and stand still whilst we prepare you."

Jorian stood up, and they began to undress him. They took off his Irazi cap, unbuttoned his vest and shirt, and untied the draw string of his trousers. Jorian soon stood in his breechclout, which one of the girls began to unfasten.

"*Eek!*" said Jorian. "Ladies, please!"

"Oh, but this, too, must come off!" said a priestess with a giggle. "Surely a man of Your Majesty's age and experience..."

"Oh, very well," grumbled Jorian. "I am an old married man, and in my native land we all bathe together. It just seemed odd."

Off came the breechclout. The appraising stares of the priestesses made Jorian wince. One said:

"Think you he will do, Gezma?"

The other priestess cocked her head thoughtfully. "He may. The gods have endowed him with length, but as for strength—well, the proof of the pudding is in the eating, they say, whilst the proof of the—"

"*Ahem!*" said Jorian. "If you must discuss me as if I were a prize bull, I had rather you did it out of my hearing. Besides, it is cool for standing in one's skin."

With squeals of suppressed laughter, the priestesses draped Jorian in flame-colored gauzy robes, which they bound with a scarlet sash. They completed his raiment with a golden wreath on his head and pearl-sewn sandals on his feet.

"Oh, my, does he not look the very god?" said one.

"He *is!*" cried the other, sinking to her knees and touching her forehead to the floor. "Great Ughroluk!" she prayed. "Deign to look with favor upon thine humble subjects!"

"Deliver us from sin and evil!" said the other, prostrating herself likewise.

"Stretch forth thy divine hand over the pious priesthood of thine eternal consort!"

Jorian fidgeted while the two young women poured out their pleas. He did feel godlike. He certainly did not feel as if he could pass miracles to save anybody from sin and evil.

"Yes, yes, I will do my divine best," he said at last. "Now where do we...?"

The priestesses scrambled up. "Will Your Divine Majesty follow us?"

More corridors, and then he came to a chapel. One

of the priestesses whispered: "Usually the rite is held in the main sanctum, but that is full of craftsmen."

As Jorian entered, a small orchestra of lyres and pipes played a delicate, tingling melody. In the center of the room stood a huge bed. The air was heavy with incense and perfume.

Before the altar at one side stood High Priestess Sahmet. Like Jorian, she was enveloped in gauze. On her noble brow, a silver tiara flashed with white gems. In the dim light of the little oil lamps hung from the ceiling, she looked almost beautiful. As Jorian approached, she bowed low, murmuring:

"All hail, divine consort! All hail, king of the gods!"

"All hail, Your Sanctity," said Jorian. "Here is your ring, madam."

The following morning, Jorian met Karadur in King Ishbahar's palace, whither the wizard had gone to report to his royal employer. The two set out afoot for Karadur's quarters. As they passed through the Gate of Happiness, Jorian squinted up at Mazsan's head, which occupied one of the spikes atop the gate. He said:

"Some of his ideas seemed sound to me. Too bad they couldn't have been tried out. If someone could persuade the king to command them..."

"That has been tried," said Karadur. "Mazsan himself once urged Ishbahar to redistribute the lands of the great magnates amongst the peasants. But these lords are powerful men, with their own armed followings, and they would not without demur accede to the loss of their power and pelf. A hero-king might undertake it, were he willing to risk an uprising led by the magnates; but poor old Ishbahar..." The Mulvanian shrugged. "How went things last night?"

Jorian laughed. "Damndest experience of my life, and I've had some beauties." He told of his robing and his being conducted to the wedding chapel. He continued: "They made me stand for hours, clad in those gauzy things like one of the he-whores you see mincing up and down Shashtai II Street, whilst they went through an eternity of ritual. They sang hymns and intoned prayers, whereof I could understand nought, since they were in an old form of the language. They handed me a silver thunderbolt and a golden sunbeam and bade me wave them about in prescribed motions.

"Well, I am not exactly decrepit, but 'tis hard to keep up one's interest for hours—if 'interest' be the word I seek. At last the mummery was over, and Sahmet and I were hailed as the lawfully wedded god and goddess. These deities had supposedly taken up their temporary abodes within our mortal frames."

"Felt you any divine possession?" asked Karadur.

"Nary a bit. Belike the true Ughroluk and Nubalyaga were otherwise occupied. Or, belike, when they feel like a bit of amorous libration, they can do it perfectly well in their own persons without employing mortals as surrogates.

"Anyway, Sahmet led me to the bed. I was taken aback by the thought of futtering the dame with all the company looking on bug-eyed. I wondered if I could— ah—rise to the occasion under those circumstances. But the priestesses hauled out screens, which they set up around the bed, and snuffed all but one of the lamps. I heard them swishing out of the chamber, and then the only sound was that of that damned orchestra, tweetling and plunking away in the corner.

"Well, even when I had a harem in Xylar, I never invited in the Royal Band to play whilst I plumbed the depths. I may be old-fashioned, but for some things I like privacy. Howsomever, necessity is a stern schoolmaster and Sahmet, a handsome woman. So I set about my business, with the usual kissing and fondling and disrobing. Presently we were one flesh, as say the preachers."

"How fared you?"

"Wherefore would you know, old ascetic? The details would shock your pure soul."

"Indulge my curiosity, my son. All human affairs are of moment to me, even though my spiritual profession limits my participation in worldly activities. Of course, such things are of but abstract concern to me, who must needs conserve his chastity to attain the highest levels of magical practise. But my knowledge of amatory matters is all gained at second hand, from books, and you can furnish knowledge the books overlook."

"Very well. The first try was not very successful. As a result of my year of virtuous conduct, I was like a crossbow on a hair trigger. Sahmet was disappointed, but I told her not to worry; that with a respite I should be able to repeat my performance.

"So, for the next half-hour, we ate and drank and talked of this and that. I told her of some of the deeds of King Fusinian. Then I was ready again, and this time I did a proper fifty-stroke job. The lady flopped beneath me like a fish on a hook. She said it was the first time in years that she had really enjoyed a man; in fact, ever since she had quarreled with Chaluish.

"But think you she was then ready to drop off to sleep? By Vaisus' brazen arse, nay! She lusted for more. After another half-hour, I managed to work up another stand and gave her a proper frigging.

"But then she wanted *still* more. Becoming weary, I pretended to go to sleep, which in sooth soon became the real thing. But this morn, at the dawn's first light, I was aroused by my holy bedmate, diddling with me in hopes of raising my temple column."

"Did she succeed?"

"Oh, aye, it worked; if anything, too well." Jorian yawned. "I could sleep the clock around. Afterwards she crushed me to her ample bosom with hot words of love. She swore I should never leave Iraz but remain here for ay, to riddle her night and day."

"You could fare further and do worse," said Karadur.

"What? Become a male concubine? And give up my little Estrildis? You must think me a mere tomcat, fornicating about the world as opportunity offers."

"Nay, my son. This is, after all, the lawful consummation of a sacerdotal rite and hence no—ah—fornication."

"Not so lawful. The ram in this holy tupping is supposed to be the king, and I'm not the king. If High Priest Chaluish find out and have a mind to make trouble...No, thank you! These high intrigues are too chancy for a simple fellow like me.

"Besides, who knows what'll happen when Ishbahar dies? With all that fat, he looks not like a good risk. Then the new king and the priestess might decide to have me quietly murdered—they're skillful with poison here—to rid themselves of my awkward presence.

"In any case, whilst I may not be of the stuff of heroes, I care not to be any lady's fancy man. Futtering is good healthy fun, but I'd rather earn my bread with my hands and head than with my prick. Besides, I like it better with my own dear little wife, with whom 'tis an act of love and not of mere lust. Now I have the king's promise of the copper bathtub, all I need is a proper spell from you to make it fly. Then ho for Xylar!"

"The spell is still incomplete," said Karadur.

"Well, hurry it up! Put more men on the job!"

"When I can, I will. But just now we at the House of Learning are occupied with preparations for the grand festival that the king has commanded for five days hence, to celebrate the salvation of Iraz. If you be not too busy with your clocks, I could employ your engineering skills at the House, in the designs of some of our stage effects."

"Glad to help," said Jorian.

IX

THE WAXEN WIFE

As GUESTS OF THE KING, JORIAN AND KARADUR FOL-
lowed Ishbahar's litter up the ramp to the royal box.
At the top of the ramp, the litter bearers set the litter
down. This time, the bearers were slaves—hairy ape-
men from the jungles of Komilakh—not aristocrats.
King Ishbahar did not trust his poundage to amateurs
on such slopes.

The king wriggled out of the litter like a broaching
whale. He waved to the crowd and puffed through the
entrance to his box, around which guardsmen were
drawn up. Jorian and Karadur followed.

"Sit anywhere you like, our dear fellows, anywhere
you like!" said the king. "We needs must occupy this
cursed throne, albeit it is far from comfortable. Now,
where is lunch? Ah, steward, here you are! Doctor Karadur, will you move your chair, pray, to let the table
be set up? Master Jorian, we have a real treat for you:
minced scarlet monkey from Beraoti, fried in the fat of
the giant tortoise of Burang. And wine made from the
chokeberry of Salimor. Try it!"

Jorian thought that chokeberry wine was an excellent name for the fluid, but he drowned his potion. The
king leaned confidentially towards him. "Are you in
fine fettle today, dear boy?"

"As far as I know, sire. Why?"

"We have a little surprise for you later. We are sure
that so stalwart a youth as yourself would hardly shriek
and swoon with shock; but we thought it well to warn
you."

"May I ask the nature of this—"

"Nay, you may not!" The king gave Jorian a heavy wink. "To tell you now were to spoil the fun, heh heh. You shall see in good time—in good time. Do you dance?"

"I dance some Novarian dances, like the volka and the whirligig. Why, sire?"

"We are planning a grand ball. You can doubtless learn the Penembic steps. It has been years since we gave one; as you can see, dancing is not exactly our forte."

While the king shoveled in the food, and Jorian and Karadur ate modest portions, the stands below them filled. As before, the Pants sat on their left in blue and gold, while the Kilts, in red and white, sat on their right. Nobles and officials occupied the intermediate strip.

"Let us hope that we have not another factional disturbance," said Karadur.

The king swallowed a huge mouthful. "We had the stasiarchs before us just this morning, Doctor. We laid down the law to them, we assure you! They promised to love each other like brothers. Like brothers, they said."

"Brotherly love, sire, cannot always be counted upon," said Jorian, "as in the case of the kings Forimar and Fusonio of my native Kortoli."

"What is this tale, Master Jorian?" asked the king.

"It is called the Tale of the Waxen Wife. King Forimar was a collateral ancestor of the better-known King Filoman the Well-Meaning, who was the father of King Fusinian the Fox. This king was known as Forimar the Esthete. He was noted for his indifference to public affairs and for his passion for the arts, at which he was himself no mean performer. He was a fair architect, an accomplished musician, a worthy composer, a fine singer, and an excellent painter. Some of his poems are the glories of Kortolian literature to this day. He could not, alas, do all these things and at the same time run the kingdom.

"As a result of Forimar's neglect, public affairs in

Kortoli got into a frightful mess. The army was a cowardly rabble, crime and corruption prevailed in the city, and the people were on the verge of revolt. Then the army of neighboring Aussar marched into Kortoli. The city was saved by a ruse devised by Forimar's brother Fusonio, who returned in the nick of time from a mission abroad.

"In saving the city, however, Fusonio demanded as his price that Forimar abdicate in his favor. This Forimar did with ill grace; but I will tell Your Majesty that story some other time.

"Anyway, the king was now Fusonio, who was of a very different character. Fusonio had none of his brother's esthetic sensitivities. He was a bluff, hearty, sensual type, whose idea of a large evening was to spend it incognito in some low tavern frequented by the rougher element, swilling ale and roaring ribald songs with unwashed peasants and ruffianly muleteers.

"Whereas Forimar was unwedded, Fusonio had a plump, peasantly, and not at all beautiful wife, named Ivrea, who had borne him five children. The twain would oft argue familial matters at the tops of their voices until the windows rattled; but woe betide the man who thought they were really quarreling and sought to take advantage of the fact! Both would turn upon him like tigers, and the children like tiger cubs.

"After his abdication, Forimar at first found it a relief not to be pestered by his ministers for decisions about public works, and hiring and firing, and foreign affairs, and law and order, and all those other tedious matters that take up a ruler's time."

"We know whereof you speak," said King Ishbahar.

"After a while, however, Forimar began to regret his lost kingship. Whilst his brother granted him an ample stipend, it was no longer enough to enable him to gratify his artistic whims. For ensample, he had an idea for an all-Novarian poetry contest, which he hoped to make into an annual affair and thus to place Kortoli in the front rank as a cultural center. As usual, he entertained grandiose ideas for the prizes. He had already spent his allowance on paintings, sculptures, and the like and had borrowed against it until his credit was exhausted. When he besought of his brother ten thousand golden marks for poetry prizes, Fusonio told him he was out of his mind.

" 'I have enough trouble rounding up tax money to repair the damages of your reign, dear brother,' quoth he. 'Get you gone and contemplate the beauty of a daisy in the field, or something equally cheap and harmless. You shall get no money for your schemes here, unless you save up your emolument.'

"It happened that a man named Zevager had lately set up an exhibition of waxworks in Kortoli City, showing such historical tableaux as King Finjanius defying the priests, the crowning of Ardyman the Terrible as emperor of Novaria, and the beheading of the rebel Roskianus. Zevager, who prided himself on the meticulous realism and authenticity of his exhibits, besought the former king to allow such an effigy to be made of His Highness and displayed. Forimar, who had never shown any sense about money but was now straitened by its lack, demanded a fee, which Zevager paid.

"Forimar took an interest in making the image, as he did in all the arts. Thus he discovered that Zevager, besides the usual techniques of making waxen effigies, knew something of magic. He cast a glamor spell upon the image, so that it looked even more like its living model then it otherwise would have. Forimar went to the Bureau of Commerce and Licenses and learnt that Zevager had no license to practise magic in Kortoli. This gave him a handle to use in dealing with the man.

"When the exhibit of the waxen Forimar proved popular, Forimar subtly insinuated into Zevager's mind the thought of making images of King Fusonio and Queen Ivrea. For a larger bribe, Forimar undertook to gain the permission of the royal couple to having their images put on display. He said it would cost him vast sums in bribes and contributions to worthy causes favored by his brother; but in fact it cost him nought. He simply asked his brother and sister-in-law at breakfast whether they would mind if he told his old friend Zevager that he might reproduce them in wax.

" 'Not at all,' said Fusonio, 'so long as his images do not make monsters of us. It will be good public relations.'

"Thus Forimar kept all the money that Zevager paid him, but he was still far short of the ten thousand marks needed for his poetry contest. So he became more and more intimate with Zevager. Soon he enticed the showman into a conspiracy against the throne. He inveigled the magician into his plot by, on one hand, dangling before him the post of Minister of Fine Arts when Forimar should become king, and on the other hinting that, if Zevager resisted his lure, he would denounce the showman for witchcraft or unlawful magic.

"In his magical arsenal, Zevager had a spell of immobility. To effect this spell, he had to get samples of Fusonio's hair and finger-nail parings. Forimar got these for him.

"One night, when Fusonio was out on one of his pub-crawls, Zevager cast the spell upon him as he was passing near the waxwork museum. Zevager and Forimar dragged the statuesque Fusonio within, exchanged his garments with those on the waxwork, and set him up in place of the image. The effigy they hid in a lumber room.

"Then Forimar hastened to the palace, awoke his sister-in-law, and gave her a document in his brother's writing. The document stated:

"My darling Ivrea:
    I have departed the kingdom for a secret meeting of all the heads of Novarian city-states in Xylar City, about threatening moves by the nomads of Shven. My absence should be kept quiet as long as possible. Meanwhile, my brother Forimar is named regent. Convey my love to the children and promise them that I shall be back in a fortnight or two.

Fusonio Rex

"Actually, the document was a clever forgery. Being an artist, Forimar could feign the calligraphy of anyone

142

he chose. Ivrea was startled; but the tale sounded plausible, since there had been rumors of an invasion from Shven.

"So Forimar ascended the throne as regent. His first act was to announce his poetry contest and appoint a committee of judges. He entered no poems of his own, knowing that he would have an unfair advantage in such a contest. This would militate against making the contest a respected annual event. He was sincere in his desire to advance the art of poetry and to promote Kortoli as a center of culture.

"Forimar's next act was to begin a purge of his brother's adherents. He retired some, sent others to far places, and demoted still others. The posts thus vacated he filled with his own supporters. He moved cautiously, not wishing to arouse suspicion. He calculated that in a month, when Fusonio was due to return, he would have the machinery of state firmly in his grip and could declare himself king.

"As for Fusonio, now standing regally in Zevager's waxworks, Forimar would decide what to do with him later. He hesitated to slay his brother, since the family had an old tradition of presenting a united front to the world despite their internal differences. On the other hand, he knew his brother for a much abler man than he, who if left alive would surely devise means to usurp the throne from the usurper.

"He reckoned, however, without Queen Ivrea. When a fortnight had passed with no word of Fusonio, she became suspicious. She besought the aid of a scryer, who sent his mystic vision to Xylar and reported that there was no sign of an international conference in that city.

"Ivrea mourned, sure that foul play had befallen her man but uncertain what to do next. One day, missing him, she stopped at Zevager's museum to look at his waxworks. Fusonio's effigy, she thought, were better than no husband at all. Zevager was delighted that the queen and several of her ladies should patronize his establishment. He showed them about with much bowing and scraping.

"When Ivrea sighted the ostensible effigy of Fusonio, she exclaimed at its verisimilitude. In fact, she said, she could scarce believe that it was not her man in the flesh. When Zevager was talking to some of the other women at the other end of the chamber, she touched the hand of the image and found that it did not feel like wax.

"Then she conceived a daring plan. She made careful note of the costume on her own effigy.

"Back in the palace, she supped that even with her brother-in-law. 'I met your friend Master Zevager today,' she said, and artlessly told of her visit. 'He said something about seeing you there tomorrow.'

"'Oh?' said Forimar. 'Methought it was the day after tomorrow—but then, I always get dates mixed up.'

"That night, Ivrea sallied forth with a single guardsman whom she trusted and another fellow lately released from gaol for burglary. For a suitable reward, the burglar picked the lock on the door of Zevager's museum, admitted her, and locked the door behind her. Ivrea climbed the stair to the loft where the images stood. Clad almost exactly like the waxwork, she hid the effigy of herself behind a curtain and took its place.

"When sounds announced the approach of Zevager and his first customers, she stiffened to immobility. One of the viewers said that the image of the queen was so lifelike that she could swear she saw it breathe. Luckily, Zevager took this as a compliment to his glamor spell.

"Later, when there were no regular customers in the museum, Regent Forimar arrived. Standing before the royal trio of images, he nervously asked Zevager what was up. 'Are our plans discovered?' he panted.

"'Nay, my lord, not to my knowledge,' said the showman. 'True, there have been rumors that King Fusonio set out on some mysterious quest but never reached his destination. He vanished off the earth, they say.' Zevager glanced at the effigy of the king and chuckled. 'Of course, my lord, you and I know that he is in plain sight still—if one know where to look.'

"'Hush up, you fool!' said Forimar. 'Even walls have

ears. I may have to strike sooner than I expected. Therefore we may have to scrap one of your waxen images.' He in his turn looked at Fusonio. 'A pity, but we cannot risk having him turn up alive and vigorous.'

"The twain walked slowly down the loft, talking in low voices, so that Queen Ivrea could no longer hear them. But she knew enough. Zevager saw his royal guest out and came back up the stairs.

"As he stepped out on the floor of the loft, a movement made him turn. He had just time to glimpse the queen's effigy, as he thought, swinging the ax from the tableau of the execution of Roskianus the rebel. He gave one horrified shriek ere the blade split his skull. Luckily for Ivrea, who was a strapping wench, the ax in the tableau was real and not an imitation of painted wood. Zevager had prided himself on authenticity.

"The showman's apprentice was at the door below to collect admission fees. When he heard the disturbance, he hurried up the stairs. When he saw Ivrea with a bloody ax in her hand and Zevager lying dead, he gave an even louder shriek and took to his heels.

"With the death of Zevager, the spell he had cast upon Fusonio quickly wore off. The king blinked and rubbed his eyes and began to breathe normally.

"'Where am I?' he said. 'What in the forty-nine Mulvanian hells is going on?'

"When things had been explained, he said 'Hand me the ax, my dear. My reach is longer than yours.' And the pair marched post-haste back to the palace. The guards gaped at the sight of their king and queen approaching the palace unescorted, the king with a bloody ax on his shoulder; but none barred their way.

"Presently Fusonio came upon his brother, practising a flute solo in his study. Seeing what was toward, Forimar fell to his knees and begged for his life.

"'Well,' said Fusonio, swinging the bloody ax about his head, 'I ought to give you what our ancestor gave Roskianus. No headless man has ever yet caused his sovran trouble.

"'But then, we have our tradition of keeping a united front to the world, which I am loath to breach. So you shall depart forthwith as my ambassador to Salimor in the Far East. And I shall send a message to my old friend the Sophi of Salimor, that if he is fain to keep our profitable trade, he must hold you there for the rest of your days.'

"And so it was done. Face was saved by the appointment of Forimar as ambassador, none but a very few knowing that he was going into exile and genteel captivity. It is said that he wrought revolutions in several of the native arts of Salimor, but that I cannot vouch for."

"What of Forimar's poetry contest?" asked the king.

"Since the judges had been chosen, the announcements had been made, and the submissions were already pouring in, Fusonio forbore to cancel the event, lest in so doing he dishonor the government of Kortoli and bring to light the discord betwixt him and his brother. A few sennights later, after Forimar's departure, the judges announced their awards. First prize, they said, should go to Vatreno of Govannian for his poem, *Demonic Downfall*. This verse began:

> "Temper the bejeweled interpleading,
> Monotheistic, fair, letter-perfect;
> Counterchange an alien thither.
> We prevaricate, junket despumate,
> And traverse plumate lanes.
> Intercommunication is pixilated.
> Explanation: liquoricity incorrigible...

"The judges brought the manuscripts of all the prizewinning poems to King Fusonio for his approval. He was supposed to bestow the prizes the following day. Fusonio read Vatreno's poem and said:

"'What is this? Some kind of joke?'

"'Oh, no, Your Majesty,' quoth the chief judge. 'It is a serious poem, very soul-revealing.'

"'But,' said Fusonio, 'the thing has neither rhyme nor rhythm. Moreover, meseems it makes no sense. It is not my idea of a poem at all.'

146

"'Oh, that!' said the judge. 'One can see that Your Majesty, with all due respect, has not kept up with late developments in the art of poesy. Rhyme and rhythm have been abandoned as archaic, artificial fetters on the artist's creativity.'

"'But still, one expects a poem to make sense!'

"'Not today, sire; one does not. We live in chaotic times, so poetry should reflect the chaos of the times. If the world fail to make sense, one cannot expect a poem to do so.'

"'Perhaps you feel chaotic, messires,' said the king, 'but I do not. In fact, to me the world makes very good sense indeed.'

"'Would that your humble servants had Your Majesty's divine omniscience!' said the chief judge with sarcasm.

"'I claim no omniscience,' said Fusonio with ominous calm. 'The world is far too complicated for any one mortal mind to encompass in its entirety. The few things I do claim to understand seem to follow orderly natural laws—including the follies of my fellow men.' He flicked the paper with a finger. 'If you ask me, Master Vatreno composed this thing by opening a dictionary at random and pointing to words with his eyes closed.'

"'Well, ah,' said the judge, 'as a matter of fact, sire, that is just what he did. Afterwards he added a few auxiliary words like "the" to give it grammatical form. We thought it a brilliant poetical innovation. It is the coming thing.'

"Fusonio glanced through the poems to which the judges had awarded the lesser prizes, but they pleased him no more than did *Demonic Downfall*. At last he said:

"'And I am supposed to pay ten thousand good marks out of my straitened treasury for this garbage! Well, when I order beer in a tavern, I at least expect beer for my coin and not horsepiss.' With that, he tore the manuscripts across with one wrench and roared: 'Get out, you dolts! Asses! Noodleheads!'

"The judges ran from the chamber with their robes flying and King Fusonio after them, thwacking their

147

rumps with his scepter. The poetry contest was called off on the ground that nought worthy of award had been submitted. This act caused much discontent among the artists and the advanced thinkers, who called Fusonio a low-browed tyrant and a crass vulgarian. But Fusonio paid no heed and had, in fact, a long and successful reign."

King Ishbahar laughed heartily. "Luckily for us, perhaps, we have no brothers; nor has poetry in Penembei ever reached such a pitch of refinement that none but the poet can ever understand one of his own compositions. But now the program is due to begin." To his secretary he said: "Herekit, hand us our reading glass and the proclamation."

Ishbahar stood up and read, while the crier bellowed his words through the speaking trumpet. The speech was the usual amass of clichés, and then the parades and clownings and races began.

X

THE CROWN OF PENEMBEI

THE WESTERN HALF OF THE HIPPODROME WAS IN SHADOW when the last race had been run. King Ishbahar stood up to announce the winners. As before, the crier relayed his words.

"Leave not early, good people," said the king. "When the formalities are over, we shall have somewhat to say that will interest you."

The king went down the list of winners. As the crier called each name, the winner marched up the steps to the royal box, bent the knee, and, to general applause, received his prize from the king. For once, the rivalry of the Pants and the Kilts seemed in abeyance.

Then King Ishbahar cleared his throat. "Loyal subjects of the Penembic crown!" he said. "Amidst the turmoils of the last month, we have been delayed in bringing up a matter of moment to all of you: to wit, the succession.

"You are all aware that we have no heirs of our body, legitimate or otherwise, living. Therefore, as our reign nears its destined end, it behooves us, to assure an orderly succession, either to search amongst our more distant kinsmen for a suitable candidate or to resort to the extreme measure of adoption.

"Be not astonished at the mention of adoption, our friends. True, the succession has not passed by adoption for over a century. But some may have forgotten that the great King Hoshcha was an adopted son of his predecessor, Shashtai the Third. Hoshcha had not a drop of the blood of Juktar the Great in his veins. To retain

149

the crown within our divine family, he wedded both of his predecessor's daughters, and the first of their sons to reach maturity was his successor.

"Now we are confronted by a similar situation. True, we have living male relatives, but amongst them we have failed to find any who qualify for the duties of king.

"The gods, however, have sent us a true hero—a man young enough to give the throne many years of vigorous occupancy, yet old enough to be past his youthful follies; a man of mighty thews, active mind, and solid character. He has already saved holy Iraz from the horde of miscreants who lately assailed her. Moreover, the fatidical and astrological indications agree that he was born on a lucky day.

"We have, therefore, this day signed and sealed the documents adopting this hero as our son and designating him as our lawful successor. Anon, we shall arrange for his marriage to one or more of our kinswomen, amongst whom are several of nubile age and winsomeness.

"This done, we shall abdicate the throne in favor of our adopted son, ere the holy father Chaluish find it needful to wait upon us with the sacred rope."

Sounds of disturbance began to swell from the throng.

"Nay, nay, good people," said the king, "be not surprised at talk of abdication! Jukar II did it, as historical records attest. Quiet, please! Quiet! We have not yet told you the name of our chosen successor."

Jorian, having inferred what was coming next, gave Karadur a desperate glare. The old Mulvanian only spread his hands helplessly.

"The hero in question," continued Ishbahar, "my adopted son and your next king, is Jorian the son of Evor! Rise, my son!"

Leaning towards Karadur, Jorian hissed: "*Oi!* Get me out of this, curse it!"

"I cannot," murmured Karadur. "I was surprised, also. Stand up as the king commands!"

"But I don't wish to be king—"

"Later, later. Stand up now!"

Jorian stood up. A slight pattering of applause was quickly drowned in a storm of boos and catcalls. From the benches occupied by the Pants arose a chant, growing louder with each repetition: "Dirty foreigner! Dirty foreigner! *Dirty foreigner!* DIRTY FOREIGNER!"

On the other side, the Kilts took up the cry until the Hippodrome rocked with it. The stasiarchs, Vegh and Amazluek, could be seen standing amid their factions, beating time like orchestra conductors. The chant spread to the rest of the audience until it became deafening.

King Ishbahar stood beside Jorian with tears running down his fat cheeks. "P-pray, good subjects—" he stammered. The crier shouted his words but was unheard in the din of "Dirty foreigner."

Missiles began to fly. Royal guardsmen rushed towards the royal box to protect the king. Colonel Chuivir appeared at the rear of the box.

"Your Majesty!" he shouted. "Come quickly, or all is lost! The factions have united in sedition against your throne. You must get back to your palace!"

"Come, our friends," said Ishbahar to Jorian and Karadur. The king waddled out of the box to the top of the ramp. His gilded litter lay, smashed, on one side.

"How shall we return to the palace without a conveyance?" he quavered.

"Walk!" said Chuivir.

Another guardsman rushed up clanking and spoke into the colonel's ear. Beyond the crowd of gleaming guardsmen, Jorian glimpsed a scud of mob, missiles flying, and weapons whirling. Chuivir said:

"The insurgents have seized the waterfront of Zaktan. Your Majesty will have to use Hoshcha's Tunnel."

"Must we climb that dreadful hill afoot?"

"It is that, or else," said the colonel with visible impatience.

"Ah, us! Let us hasten, then."

Followed by Jorian and Karadur and protected by a mass of guardsmen, the king puffed his way down the ramp. In the concourse, screams of rage and defiance and a rain of cobblestones, bricks, potsherds, and other missiles assailed the guardsmen. A knot of citizens rushed at the guards with clubs and knives. The guards easily beat off the attack, leaving a wrack of tumbled bodies. A few guards who bore crossbows began methodically shooting into the swirling, screaming crowds.

"This way!" yelled Chuivir.

Stumbling over corpses, they pushed across the street surrounding the Hippodrome and started up the slope to the Temple of Nubalyaga. After a few steps, the king halted, panting.

"We can no more," he moaned.

"Help me with him, Master Jorian," said the colonel.

Each of them draped one of the king's fat arms around his neck. With help on either side, the king dragged his monstrous weight slowly up the hill.

At the top, the eunuch guard was already drawn up behind their gate with crossbows ready. They opened the gate to admit the king and his escort.

At the temple, High Priestess Sahmet came running out. After a quick explanation, she said: "Follow me, sire!" and led the way towards the Tunnel of Hoshcha.

"Hold!" cried Colonel Chuivir. "I shall come with you as soon as I appoint a commander of the local detachment."

"Why?" asked the king.

"If I can regain the palace and take command of the main body of the Guard, belike I can keep the sedition from spreading across the river. Captain Saloi!"

"Aye, sir?"

"Take command of the guardsmen in Zaktan. Try to guard the main points, like this temple. If you have enough men, send a flying squad to patrol and break up gatherings of rebels." He turned to the king. "If it please Your Majesty, we are ready to go now."

Sahmet clutched Jorian's arm and whispered: "You shall see me again at the next full moon!"

Four men moved through the Tunnel of Hoshcha: Jorian in front, bearing a lanthorn; then King Ishbahar, puffing and panting; then Karadur; and lastly Colonel Chuivir, with another lanthorn. To Jorian it seemed an eternity, for the king toddled along with tiny steps at a snail's pace.

They had come, he supposed, halfway across and were under the deepest part of the Lyap, when he saw something that made his hair rise. From the side of the tunnel, a tiny jet of water sprayed out, shooting halfway across at waist height before breaking up into discrete drops.

"Gods and goddesses!" he exclaimed. "Look at that, Karadur!"

"Here is another," said the wizard, pointing to the overhead, whence another trickle of water descended.

Everywhere they looked, forward and back, water appeared in drips and leaks and spurts. The floor of the tunnel became wet and slippery.

"What befalls, Doctor Karadur?" wheezed the king. "Have your hydrophobic spells failed? Should we have ordered pumps installed after all?"

"It must be," said Karadur, "that a mob has invaded the House of Learning and snatched my wizards Goelnush, Luekuz, and Firaven from their task. I hope they have not done the poor fellows to death."

"Yes, yes," said Jorian. "But hadn't we better hurry, ere this burrow fill with water?"

"Aye, my son, that we must." Karadur turned back. "Your Majesty—"

"We—are going (*puff*)—as fast—as we can," said the king. "If you fear drowning—go on—without us."

"Oh, come on, sire!" said Chuivir heartily. "Lengthen those royal strides!"

With every step, the leakage of water increased. Soon the four were splashing along ankle-deep. Groaning and gasping, the king made a desperate effort to speed up his uncouth waddle. Then he slipped and fell with a great splash.

"Your Majesty!" cried the three others at once.

Jorian and Karadur handed Chuivir their lanthorns. Grunting with effort, they got Ishbahar into a sitting position. The king's eyes were half closed, and his breath came in rattling snores. He did not answer at first. They pushed him so that his back rested against the side wall of the tunnel. The water was calf-deep.

At last the king opened his eyes. "Master Jorian!" he whispered.

"Aye, sire?"

"Lean over. Close."

Jorian leaned. With a last effort, the king reached up, plucked the serpent crown from his bewigged pate, and clapped it on Jorian's head.

"Now—my boy—you are king. These witnesses..."

The king's voice trailed off to a mumble and ceased. Karadur tried to feel his pulse.

"I cannot locate the blood vessel through all that fat," he grumbled. He thrust a hand inside the king's robe and then laid his ear against the king's breast.

"He is dead," said Karadur. "Methinks his heart succumbed."

"Not surprising, with all that blubber," said Jorian.

"Let us be off, Captain—ah—sire," said Chuivir, "ere we drown like rats."

"What of the king?" said Jorian. "It would look odd for him to have entered the tunnel with us but not to emerge. An we cannot show his unmarked body, men will say we slew him."

"You are right, my son," said Karadur. "Help Jorian to bear the body, Colonel."

Chuivir took an arm. "Take the other, Master—ah— King Jorian."

The two struggled and heaved. Between them, they got the body up. Grunting, they staggered a few steps. Then Jorian slipped. The two men and the corpse fell with a mighty splash. Karadur said:

"If the water become any deeper, the body will float. You two can haul it by the feet."

"O wise old man!" said Jorian. "Take his other ankle, Chuivir."

The water was soon knee-deep. Karadur, with his robe hiked up to his bony brown knees, went ahead. He held the two lanthorns, which gave off feeble yellow glows. Behind him waded Jorian and Chuivir, hauling on the body's ankles. The corpse still scraped along the floor of the tunnel, but with each rise in the water level, the body lightened.

"Are you sure we have the right tunnel?" said Chuivir. "We must have walked halfway to the Fediruni border."

"This is the tunnel, certes," said Jorian. "It is now sloping up. If we can keep ahead of the rise in the water level, we shall escape."

"The water gains," said Chuivir. "It is up to my waist. Would I had doffed this damned armor in the temple."

The deepening water floated the king's body off the floor and made it easy to tow. On the other hand, it impeded the movements of the three living men. They could only plod, plod under a continuous shower of jets and leaks and trickles from the parts of the tunnel not yet submerged.

"That is the trouble with magic," growled Jorian. "When folks think they can count on it, they skimp on proper engineering and maintenance."

The water continued to rise; it was now breast-high. Jorian and Chuivir tried to speed their progress by making swimming motions with their free arms. Karadur, being smaller, was forced to hold the lanthorns over his head to keep them from being drowned. His white beard trailed in the water.

A spurt of water from the overhead struck one of the lanthorns, which went out with a faint hiss. On they plodded through the gloom. Jorian mutered:

"Any higher, and the cursed corpse will scrape the roof."

"If the remaining light go, at least we can feel our way," panted Chuivir. "There are no forks or branches in this tunnel, are there?"

"Nay," said Karadur. "It runs straight to—*glub!*" The water had been up to his chin, and a ripple filled his mouth. He coughed and sputtered, shaking the remaining lanthorn.

"Ho, don't put out our last light!" said Jorian. "Drowning is bad enough, but drowning in the dark..."

"Save your breath, King" said Chuivir.

Karadur, who had gained a little on the other two, turned back long enough to say: "When my boy Jorian ceases conversing, you will know he has terminated his present incarnation."

"Can you talk without getting a mouthful of water?" said Jordan.

"Now that you mention it, the water has not deepened recently."

The water level remained constant for a time, while the only sounds in the tunnel were the heavy breathing of the three men and the splashing of their slow progress. At last the water began to recede. Soon the king's body was again scraping the bottom.

"At least, we are now above the river level," said Jorian. "Now all we need worry about is being slaughtered by rebels at the far end."

"I could not fight a mouse," groaned Chuivir.

Karadur knocked on the secret door to the king's bedchamber. When he had explained, the door opened. After some delay, several guards and palace servants came down the stair with a stretcher.

They found Jorian and Chuivir a furlong down the tunnel, sitting in half a foot of water with their backs to the wall, breathing heavily in a state of utter exhaustion. The monstrous corpse lay in the water near them.

When the people from the palace had rolled the body on the stretcher, tied it fast with straps, and borne it back up the tunnel, Jorian got to his feet with a groan. Chuivir, weighed down by his armor, had to be helped up. After another struggle, the two crept on hands and knees up the stair and entered the royal bedchamber. They collapsed into chairs and lay back, dripping puddles on the floor. Karadur already occupied another chair, with his turban on the floor beside him. The wizard's eyes were closed.

"Wine!" croaked Jorian. Servants scurried.

Jorian looked up from his goblet to see an officer of

the Guard. "Sir!" said this man. "What means this? King Ishbahar is dead, and you wear his crown!"

"Do I, forsooth?" said Jorian. He pulled off the serpent crown and stared at it absently, as if he had never seen it before.

"Is it true what they say, that His late Majesty named you his sucessor?"

"It is," said Chuivir behind the officer. "His Majesty died of natural causes in the tunnel whilst fleeing the insurrection in Zaktan. Have the rebels attacked the palace yet?"

"Nay, Colonel. But some have crossed the river, and there is fighting and looting and arson along the waterfront. What are my orders?"

"Secure the palace against attack, first of all. I shall be with you presently to take active command. Now leave us. You servants, also." When the chamber had been cleared of all save Karadur, Jorian, and Chuivir, the last set down his goblet.

"Excellent wine," he said. "Vindine, methinks. I begin to feel like a human being again. Now, sir, you and I have some matters to straighten out."

"At your service, Colonel," said Jorian, also putting down his goblet.

He looked speculatively at Chuivir, wondering what chance he would have against the colonel in a fight. Chuivir wore armor and a sword against Jorian's mere dagger; but Chuivir had been much more exhausted by the ordeal in the tunnel.

Chuivir: "Do you really intend to exercise your kingship, in view of the general revolt against you?"

"No longer than I must," said Jorian. "I wanted no crown. Ishbahar was a fool to name me without first making sure of political support for the move."

"A well-intentioned wight, but no monarch," said Chuivir. "Well, that relieves my mind. You may be the lawful sovran; but as a foreigner you are unpopular. Even if I threw my full weight behind you, I know not if I could keep you on your throne. How long is no longer than you must?"

157

"As long as it takes Doctor Karadur and me to take off in our flying bathtub."

"Eh? What is this?"

"Ishbahar promised me that great copper tub of his as an aërial vehicle."

"How will you make it fly?"

Jorian nodded towards Karadur, who was rewinding his turban. "The good doctor has in his ring a demon, who will bear us aloft."

"But, Jorian!" protested Karadur. "I told you I did not wish to liberate Gorax save in direst emergency, since this will be his last labor—"

Jorian snorted. "If this be not a dire emergency, with the whole city buzzing about our ears, then I know not an emergency when I see it. Wouldst rather be torn to bits by a mob whipped up to hatred of foreigners?"

"Oh. But, my son, think of all the good you could effect if you retained the crown! You could introduce those reforms that Mazsan preached. You could provide the House of Learning with adequate financial support—"

"Not when half the people I saw would wish to shoot, stab, or poison me. They've made it plain that they want no foreigner for king. This must be that 'second crown' whereof Nubalyaga warned me in the dream. The first was the crown of Xylar, which you and I buried near the Marshes of Moru."

"The Irazis would soon forget their xenophobia," persisted Karadur, "one you were firmly ensconced in power and demonstrated what a good king you could be and how well you adapted to their ways. You already speak better Penembic than I do. After all, Juktar the Great was not only a foreigner but also a barbarian, and this is a cosmopolitan city."

Jorian shook his head. "I tried to show the Xylarians what a good king I could be, too, but that didn't stop them from trying to cut off my head. Besides, how should I ever get firmly ensconced in power, without some foreign mercenary army at my back?"

"Surely there are loyal elements in the Guard and

in the Frontier Army on whom you could rely. Once you dompted the factions—"

"And suppose I did, then what? Spend my life humping Her Sanctity Sahmet until the priests arrived with the sacred rope? No, thank you!"

"You could abolish that custom, as did that Kortolian king."

"Doubtless. But 'tis useless to try to argue me round, old man. I've had my taste of kinging it. Whilst 'twas fun in a way, I have no wish to go back to it. Many lust for the wealth, power, and glory that kingship entails, but I harbor no such lordly ambitions. A simple life, with a respectable trade, a snug house, plenty to eat and drink, a loving family, and congenial cronies will suffice me.

"Nor do I covet an Irazi wife. I already have one spouse, and that's a plenty. Besides, the more I travel, the better I appreciate my native land.

"Oh, some like the mountains, rugged and grim,
Where the sleet storms howl and the low clouds
    skim,
And you hang by your toes from a ledge's rim,
But I'll warble a rondeau and carol a hymn
    To Novaria, dear Novaria.

"And some seek the desert, barren and dry,
Where the hot sun hangs in a cloudless sky
And your camel sways and your eyeballs fry,
But I to the land of my birth will hie:
    To Novaria, my Novaria.

"While some love the spires of vast Iraz
And admire its domes with oh's and ah's
And go to the races to shout hurrahs,
But the bonniest land that ever there was
    Is Novaria, fair Novaria.

"So let the factions fight it out; 'tis no affair of mine. To the forty-nine Mulvanian hells with the Penembic crown! I'm for Xylar to rescue my little darling, and that's that."

Looking worried, Chuivir passed a hand across his forehead. "Well then, sire, I wonder—ah—perhaps you can advise me. With you gone, the leading contenders for the crown will be the stasiarchs. But I deem neither Vegh nor Amazluek a man of kingly quality; whiles, of the late king's sister's sons, one is a wastrel and the other a halfwit. General Tereyai, to whom I have sent messengers, is old and soon to retire. Admiral Kyar is dead. Have you any thought as to whom I should back?"

Jorian stared at Chuivir. "Why not be king yourself? Methinks you would make not a bad one."

Chuivir's mouth fell open. "Really? You offer *me* the crown?"

"Why not? I thought you a harmless, feckless fop, but since the rebel assault you have learnt fast."

Chuivir shrugged. "I do my poor best."

"To make it legitimate, fetch writing materials, and I will sign over the sovranty, to take effect when we leave in our flying tub. Whether you can make it good is your problem."

Chuivir rose. "I thank you, sire, and will try to deserve your trust. Now I must go to command my men; but I shall soon return to see you off."

As Chuivir clanked out, Jorian raised his voice: "Servants! Hither, pray. I want a change of clothing— warm woolens, suitable for roughing it; not these pretty silky things. And fetch a dry robe for Doctor Karadur."

"Oh, my son, I need no—"

" 'Tis cold aloft, and I can't have you catching a tisic. You there, find the chief armorer and tell him to fetch me some weapons and armor to make a choice from. And where did King Ishbahar keep his privy purse? You! Tell the cook to whip up a dinner for the doctor and me. Not fancy, but substantial, and tell him to waste no time about it."

While the servants scurried, a guardsman entered, saying: "A courier named Zerlik would fain see Your Majesty."

"Send him in," said Jorian.

The young man entered and dramatically dropped to one knee. "Your Majesty!" he cried. "I have just returned from bearing the king's letter to Othomae. Nominating you was the best thing King Ishbahar ever did. My sword is at your service; your every wish is my command!"

"That is fine, but I fear I shan't be here long enough to profit from your loyalty."

"You are leaving? Take me with you as your s-squire!"

"Alas, our vehicle cannot carry three. Colonel Chuivir is my deputy and chosen successor, so transfer your loyalty to him."

"But there must be something, sire—"

"I will tell you. You have a big house. Set aside one small room as a refuge for me, should I ever have to flee Novaria and go into hiding here."

"It shall be done! May the gods bless Your Majesty!"

"Better ask them to bless Chuivir; he will need it. Farewell!"

An hour later, the streets of Iraz resounded to the tramp of feet, the roar of mobs, the clash of arms, and the screams of the stricken. Chuivir and several of his guardsmen stood on the roof of the palace, watching the bathtub carrying Jorian and Karadur wobble off into the heavens. The rays of the setting sun gleamed redly on the copper of the tub. The vehicle shrank until it became a mere crimson spark in the deepening blue of the heavens.

Chuivir, wearing the serpent crown of Penembei instead of his helmet, sighed and murmured: "There goes the man who should really have been king, were he not debarred by popular prejudice. Ah, well." He turned to the officers around him and began to receive reports and issue commands.

About the Author

L. Sprague de Camp, who has over ninety-five books to his credit, writes in several fields: historicals, SF, fantasy, biography, and popularizations of science. But his favorite genre of literature is fantasy.

De Camp is a master of that rare animal *humorous fantasy*. As a young writer collaborating with the late Fletcher Pratt, he set forth the world-hopping adventures of Harold Shea. These are available today in two books: *The Compleat Enchanter* and *Wall of Serpents*. Together, Pratt and de Camp also wrote the delightfully zany *Tales from Gavagan's Bar*, a book which has remained in print for forty years.

In 1976, at the 34th World Science Fiction Convention, he received *The Gandalf—Grand Master Award for Lifetime Achievement in the Field of Fantasy*. The Science Fiction Writers of America presented him with their *Grand Master Nebula Award of 1978*. Alone, and with his wife and sometime collaborator Catherine, de Camp has been a welcome guest of honor at fan conventions throughout the United States.

The de Camps live in Villanova, Pennsylvania. They have two sons: Lyman Sprague, and Gerard Beekman, both of whom are distinguished engineers.

Enchanting fantasies from